Miss Carrie

A NOVEL

Miss Carrie

A NOVEL

JUDSON N. HOUT

Parkhurst Brothers Publishers
Marion, Michigan

www.parkhurstbrothers.com

Parkhurst Brothers books are distributed to the trade through the Chicago Distribution Center, and may be ordered through Ingram Book Company, Baker & Taylor, Follett Library Resources and other book industry wholesalers. To order from Chicago Distribution Center, phone 1-800-621-2736 or send a fax to 800-621-8476. Copies of this and other Parkhurst Brothers Inc., Publishers titles are available to organizations and corporations for purchase in quantity by contacting Special Sales Department at our home office location, listed on our web site. Manuscript submission guidelines for this publishing company are available at our web site.

Printed in the United States of America

First Edition, 2014

2014 2015 2016 2017 2018   12 11 10 9 8 7 6 5 4 3 2 1

 Library of Congress Cataloging in Publication Data will be available on the Publisher's web site when issued.

ISBN: Trade Paperback   978-1-62491-001-2
ISBN: e-book   978-1-62491-003-6

This book is printed on archival-quality paper that meets requirements of the American National Standard for Information Sciences, Permanence of Paper, Printed Library Materials, ANSI Z39.48-1984.

Front cover photograph and author photo: Mary Jones, MC Photography
Cover and page design: Charlie Ross
Acquired for Parkhurst Brothers Inc., Publishers by: Ted Parkhurst
Proofreaders: Bill and Barbara Paddack
042014

This novel is dedicated with abiding love

To my cherished wife,

Carolyn,

without whose support and inspiration

none of my fiction would ever have

taken root.

Acknowledgements

This novel is only possible because of the consistent love and support of my lovely wife, Carolyn, without whose encouragement I seriously doubt I would ever have attempted to write. Many, many "old ladies" have inspired me, not particularly to write, but rather to grow into a good man. These include, but are not limited to, my great-grandmother Adelia, my two grandmothers, three great aunts, four aunts, my mother-in-law and my mother, all of whom are long gone from this world, though alive daily in my memory. A great many other "old ladies" have inspired me without even knowing it. My Miss Carrie is a composite of them all. The cover model is Bobbie Sheffield of Bearden, Arkansas, who stands in elegantly for all those capable, gracious women. Thanks to Mary Catherine Jones for her cover photo and for the author photo on the back cover. Deep thanks to Melissa Gordon for typing the final draft of this novel.

Ted Parkhurst, Bill and Barbara Paddack, Charlie Ross and all the good folks at Parkhurst Brothers Publishers have again proven their mettle by creating a beautiful volume from my typescript. I appreciate all of their care and labor.

I will forever owe a debt of gratitude to Lynne Rowland, Camden's longtime local bookseller, and to all of the booksellers, reviewers, librarians, and other important people who make the book industry work for authors like me across this great country.

Judson N. Hout
Camden, Arkansas
March, 2013

I was nine years old when I first met Miss Carrie. My friends and I were doing what boys usually did on Halloween in those days. It was nineteen hundred and forty one, and if war clouds were gathering we were not aware of it.

We had been running around the streets of Fabre's Bluff soaping windows, letting air out of tires and shooting off firecrackers. We even turned over an outdoor privy, but when Jody almost fell in the hole we decided to not do that anymore.

Harold had the best idea of all. We gathered up a few fairly fresh road apples, as we called horse droppings on the streets. The apples were put in a grocery bag along with wadded-up paper, placed at a front door and set on fire. Then we knocked on the door and ran. Whoever opened the door would stomp out the fire and get horse crap all over their shoes.

We got to watch as older boys took apart a buckboard wagon and carried it piece by piece to the roof of the blacksmith shop where they reassembled it.

Then Harold got his best idea. He slipped in the hen houses of several homes and gathered up a bunch of eggs. We climbed trees and pelted passing cars and wagons with eggs.

Finally, tiring of all that, we decided to knock on doors and ask for candy. In return for the candy we promised not to mess with the house.

That's when I met Miss Carrie. We didn't know her name; we just knew she lived in a gloomy old house behind

which was a bluff bank on the Ouachita River. We had
heard that it was inhabited by an old hermit witch and a
bunch of ghosts. It was the only house we refused to mess
with.

The house was surrounded by a broken-down wrought
iron fence, and the yard was full of weeds. A short path
led to a porch with tilted pillars and creaky wooden steps.
The only illumination was the full moon in the clear sky.

Harold said, "Ben, I dare you to go knock on the door."

"Shoot, naw," I replied.

Lonnie Joe said, "Shoot fire and save matches, I
double-dog dare you."

Well that was just too much. No one could back down
from a double-dog dare.

I was scared but I said, "Okay, I'll do it, but I'm runnin'
off before she opens the door."

I slowly opened the creaky old gate and carefully
walked up the path. As I climbed the five steps I was
aware of each one squeaking, and I thought I was going to
wet my pants.

As I raised my hand to knock on the door I felt
something hit me in the back and something else hit the
back of my head. I turned around just in time to attempt
to catch a third egg as it hit me square in the chest.

As all my buddies were laughing, the door flew open,
I was jerked inside, the door slammed shut; and I was
standing face to face with the old witch herself.

She was a little taller than I and very thin. Her hair

was snow white, and the skin of her face was wrinkled as was the skin on the back of her hands. Her teeth were pearly white, and I noticed the eye tooth on the left was about a quarter of an inch longer than the rest of her teeth. She was wearing a long black dress with white lace at the cuffs. Her clothes were clean. She didn't look like a witch at all but rather like a nice old lady.

She spoke first since I was too frightened to say anything. "What's your name, young man with egg all over you?"

She smiled and then laughed, and I began to relax. "I'm Ben Williams," I replied.

"Was your grandfather Benjamin Guillaume?"

"Yes ma'am, "I replied. "That's the French name for Williams. My dad had it changed to Williams because we are Americans. He said he didn't want to have people think he was French. He waited until after his dad was dead to do it. I never knew my grandpaw. He died in the First World War. He was killed in France. Daddy said it was coincidental that an American named Guillaume was killed in France."

"It certainly was," she said. "Let me introduce myself, young man. I am Miss Carrie Stephens. One of my direct ancestors was French, and his name was Jacque Fabre. They named this town after him. He came up the Mississippi River to the Ouachita and ended up here, right here where this house stands. He had a trading post here.

"But enough about me. Get your shirt off and come into the water closet with me. I need to wash the egg off your shirt and off your face and head too. You can't go home like this. What would your folks think?"

I didn't want to undress, but she insisted. "Boy, I've seen young boys without shirts before. Don't be bashful.

Here, wrap yourself in this quilt."

I did as I was told. She took me by the hand and led me into the bathroom. I had never before heard it called a water closet. She washed my face, my hair and my shirt and then said, "Come on and sit by the fire to let your hair dry. I don't want you to catch cold. We'll dry your shirt by the fire."

There was a big fire in her fireplace, and the sitting room was cozy and pleasantly decorated. The inside of the house was very nice and nothing like the outside.

"I'm going to fix some hot chocolate, Ben. Would you like a cup?"

"Yes ma'am, please, "I replied.

"You were going to play a trick on me, and your buddies played a trick on you. You all probably thought I was some old witch because I never go out. Well I'm not, but I'd just as soon let everyone think I am. Everyone but you, that is. If they think I'm an old witch in a haunted house they'll leave me alone. That's what I want.

"But you are different. You and I are going to be friends, but don't tell anyone about it. When you see those boys tomorrow, tell them I'm a mean old woman with hairy warts all over my face. Tell them I'm mean, and you just barely escaped. But you come back often. Promise me. I like you Ben. But don't tell your daddy about me. Let this be our secret."

I was fascinated by her and knew I would come back and come back often. She was nice.

By the time my shirt had dried, I was tired and sleepy. Miss Carrie watched me put the shirt on and then she gently combed my hair.

"Now get along home, Master Ben, and remember it's our secret, just yours and mine."

As I walked home alone in the dark cold night I wondered why she told me not to tell my father and didn't mention my mother. Did she know more about me than she let on?

Arriving home about midnight I found the front door unlocked as I knew it would be. We never locked our doors in those days - no need to.

Granny and Daddy were asleep – I was glad because I didn't want to lie to them or in any other way explain Miss Carrie.

Because of the excitement the events of the night had caused, sleep came with difficulty. Thoughts of Miss Carrie and her house, so rundown on the outside and so nice on the inside, kept running through my head.

Finally morning came. I was glad it was Saturday and there was no school; because fitful sleep would have made school work difficult. After breakfast with Granny I left to find my friends and look around town to see the Halloween damage.

I found Harold, Lonnie and Jody at Gilleland's Drugstore.

"Ben, boy howdy we were worried about you," said Harold. "We were afraid the old witch was gonna eat you up or something."

"Yeah," said Lonnie and Jody in unison. "What happened?"

"If you all were so worried, why didn't you call the cops or something?" I asked.

"We were scared to," said Lonnie.

"Well anyway," I said, "the old woman grabbed me and threw me down on the floor. Two mean dogs growled at me and showed me their teeth and wouldn't let me get up. The witch threw cold water on me, and some of it fell through big cracks in the floor. She said she did it to get the eggs off of me.

"Then she tied me up in a chair and made me drink some bad tasting stuff. I puked all over myself, and she threw more cold water on me. Then she let me go home, and I puked all night long."

"Good God'amighty," Harold said. "What did she look like?"

"She had long scraggly hair and hairy warts all over her face. Her teeth were dirty and cracked, and her breath smelled like shit," I replied.

"We better never mess around her place again," exclaimed Lonnie.

The others agreed, and I could barely keep from laughing.

Walking around Fabre's Bluff that November the first, we were amazed at all we saw. The windows of many stores had been soaped, some with graffiti and some with just smears of soap. Many people were gawking at the wagon atop the blacksmith's shop. Many were cussing their overturned outhouses.

We acted dumb when asked by adults what havoc we had caused.

The other boys wanted to go play basketball, but I

wanted to go see Miss Carrie. I lied and said I had to do chores for my grandmother and left.

I was fascinated by Miss Carrie. She was very nice to me; but there was something strange, even mysterious, about her. What could it be? Why was she so interested in me? For that matter, why was I so interested in her?

The old house, as I approached it, was as creepy in the daylight as it was at night. My knock was answered by a large stocky black woman with drawn back hair and many small black moles on her face. She was dressed in a long multicolored dress and smelled like lilacs.

"You got to be Ben," she said. "My name is Lounicey, but all my friends call me Sweet Pea. You and me's gonna be friends so you call me Sweet Pea too. Come on in, Miss Carrie told me you'd be comin'. She's anxious to see you."

Miss Carrie was sitting on a small couch facing the fire. She smiled when she saw me and patted the cushion for me to sit beside her.

"Sweet Pea," she said, "Master Ben likes hot chocolate. Would you get us each a cup, please, and one for you as well."

"I already done it, Miss Carrie," she replied.

When Sweat Pea brought in the tray with the cups of chocolate, Miss Carrie asked her to sit by us and join us in the drinks.

"Lounicey takes care of me, Ben. She is also my friend. She does all my business and grocery shopping around town, because I never go out. Since you are my secret friend it is best you act like you don't know her if you see her out and about."

"Yes ma'am, "I said.

Sweet Pea just winked at me and grinned.

"Miss Carrie, "I asked, "why don't you go out? You're

nice. People would like you."

"It's a long story, Ben, and I'd rather not bring that
up," she said with a slight hint of anger.

I looked at Sweet Pea, and she nodded no with her
head slightly. I knew I was never to bring that up again.

"Ben," Miss Carrie began, "Come see me often, but I
don't think you should come to the front door. Since we
are secret friends, I don't want people to see you around
here. When you come, day or night, walk the path through
the woods to the back of the house. Come to the back door
and let yourself in. You don't have to knock. Lounicey will
show you where we hide the key."

I was intrigued by her but still a little frightened. Why
so mysterious I wondered? What were her secrets?

After awhile Sweet Pea showed me out the back door
and the location of the key. As we walked toward the path
I was to take on our visits, I asked, "Sweet Pea, why is she
so strange? I think she's very nice. I think people would
like her a lot."

"Boy, that's a long story and none of your business. If
you want to be friends with her you keep those questions
to yourself. Don't bother her none with them."

I walked the path through the woods more curious
than ever but resolved to do as Lounicey said.

Over the next few weeks I visited Miss Carrie
frequently. We talked of many things but mostly about me.
Whenever I asked about her, she would change the subject
or just avoid the question. Lounicey was always nearby.

Sometimes I would slip out of my house at night by
crawling out the window in my room onto the porch roof
and climb to the ground down a mulberry tree. If the moon
was bright I always walked on the wooded path to Miss
Carrie's back door. If the night was dark I was afraid of
the woods and would go to the front door, first making
sure that no one was watching.

The Sunday before Thanksgiving I let myself in the
back door of her house about four in the afternoon. Miss
Carrie had fallen asleep in her chair beside the fireplace.
When I saw she was asleep I tiptoed out of the room, but
she awoke and called back.

I sat on the hearth with my back to the fire.

"Ben," she said, "tell me about your family. What does
your father do? Does your mother work or stay home and
care for you?"

"My mother is dead, Miss Carrie. My daddy is a lawyer
and also a lieutenant in the National Guard. Daddy and I
live with my grandmother, Narcissa."

"I'm sorry about your mother, Ben. Your grandmother
must be Narcissa Guillaume, your father's mother."

"Yes ma'am," I said.

"So she kept Grandpaw Benjamin's name when your
dad changed his name to Williams."

"Yes ma'am. She said it would be disrespectful to my
grandfather not to keep his name. My dad understood, but
he still wanted the American form of the name for me and
him. That's why we are Williams."

"Was your mother from here?" she asked.

"No ma'am, "I replied. "She was from Little Rock.
Daddy met her in college at Fayetteville."

"What about her parents? Do they live in Little Rock?"

"They did, but they died when their house burned

down when I was a baby."

"I'm sorry. That must have caused your mother great sadness."

"No ma'am, my mother was already dead."

"Oh, again I'm sorry," she said. "How old were you when your mother died?"

"I was little," I replied, "but can we talk about something else, please?"

"Of course, we can. How about a big piece of Lounicey's sweet potato pie with whipped cream on top?"

"Yes ma'am," I exclaimed.

She left the room and brought back a large piece of pie piled high with whipped cream. As I was eating the pie she said, "Ben, honey, what time does Narcie have Thanksgiving dinner?"

"About noon."

"Well don't eat too much, because Lounicey will have our dinner about five. I want you to come eat with us and have some more sweet potato pie."

"Okay, yes ma'am," I said.

On the way home I wondered how she knew people called my grandmother Narcie. I only told her Narcissa was her name. That was just something else for me to think about.

Granny served our Thanksgiving dinner a little before noon, because my father was going to leave early that afternoon for a long weekend of duck hunting at Stuttgart. I was glad because it would be easier for me to get away for the late afternoon meal at Miss Carrie's.

Harold and Lonnie Joe came by about two on their bicycles and asked me to go mess around with them. I told them I had the diarrhea and couldn't go. Harold said they didn't want me to mess in my britches, and they left.

A little before five, I got on my bicycle and rode to the now familiar path to Miss Carrie's. While riding through the woods I resolved to find out about Miss Carrie.

The meal was delicious. Lounicey had fixed a small turkey with all the trimmings, and the three of us sat at the big table to eat, Miss Carrie and Lounicey at the ends and me in the middle.

When we took our seats Miss Carrie said, "Lounicey, will you bless the food please?"

We bowed our heads, and Lounicey said, "Lord, bless Miss Carrie and young Ben. Thank you for blessing us with this young boy in our lives. He's done brought great joy to Miss Carrie. And please, God, keep us out of this war. Bless this food we're about to eat. In Jesus' name. Amen."

While we were eating our pie I asked, "Miss Carrie, have you ever been married?"

Lounicey gave me a dirty look and slightly shook her head no as Miss Carrie looked down toward her lap.

"No, child," she said, "I've never been married."

I thought she was about to cry so I said no more.

Riding my bike home I was more curious than ever. What was Miss Carrie hiding?

During the weekend following Thanksgiving my father had to attend National Guard maneuvers at Camp Chaffee in Fort Smith. That left me with time alone with my grandmother and also time for my friends.

"Granny," I said during lunch on Saturday, "who lives in that big old spooky house on Bluff Street? You know, the one up on the bluff bank."

"Benny-boy," (she always called me Benny-boy), "you stay away from that old house. A mean old hermit woman lives there as well as the ghost of Jacque Fabre. You know, the man they named this town after."

"Aw Granny, I don't believe in ghosts."

"Well you better. When I was a little girl I saw him looking out an upstairs window. He was more of a shadow than anything, but you could see a red head scarf and a long black mustache. It really scared me, and I never went around there again."

"But who is the old woman you told me about?" I persisted.

"Her name is Carlotta something or other. I don't know for sure. The story goes that she killed a man once but, if so, nothing was ever done about it. Now I mean it; you don't ever go around that place.

"She has some old colored woman who does all her chores and runs all her errands. She must have money – probably ill-gotten gains from old Fabre."

I asked no more, for I knew none of what Granny told me was true. Except, of course, that Miss Carrie was related to Jacque Fabre. And he must have been a good man for the town to be named after him.

I decided to make no more mention of Miss Carrie or the house to anyone, not even my father. But I knew I would go back there and go often.

Two weeks later on Sunday, December the seventh, my grandmother, father and I were eating our noon meal when there was loud banging on the door. Dad answered the door and there stood Mr. Bennett, our next door neighbor. He was quite agitated.

"Turn on your radio, Jim. The goddamned Japs have attacked Pearl Harbor. They sunk a bunch of our ships and killed a bunch of people. This means war!" And then he ran down the street to alert other houses.

Dad turned on the radio, and Mr. Bennett's story was confirmed. We listened intently as details came in.

"Mom," Dad said, "you know what this means."

"Yes," she said, but then she placed her index finger to her lips and nodded toward me.

"It's okay," Dad said, "Ben's got to find out sooner or later. It might as well be now."

"Find out what?" I asked.

"Ben," Dad said, "you know I'm in the National Guard. You know I'm an officer, a lieutenant. Our country has been attacked by the Japanese. That means we have to defend ourselves. We have to go to war and fight the Japanese and probably the Germans too. The National Guard will surely be activated and have to go fight. That means I'll have to go."

"No Daddy, I don't want you to go. My mama died. I don't want you to die too."

"Son," he said, "You don't want me to be a coward, now do you? I've got a duty to go if we are called. Maybe we won't be called, but if we are I will go. I'll be careful and be sure to come back to you when the war is over. In the meantime, you'll need to be a big boy, be a man, and take care of Granny."

There was nothing else I could say. I knew he would go. I didn't want him to. I hated the damned Japs for taking my daddy away and maybe getting him killed. I was afraid I would be an orphan.

There was an air of excitement in Fabre's Bluff the next few days. News of the war came in almost hourly. We learned that almost three thousand people were killed in the attack, and many were missing. Many of our ships were sunk.

President Roosevelt declared war on Japan, and Germany declared war on us. That was just as well because Dad said we were going to have to fight the Germans anyway.

After school Monday I slipped away before my friends caught up with me and went through the woods to Miss Carrie's. I retrieved the key from under a large chipped urn and let myself in. Lounicey was in the kitchen and winked at me as I approached. Then she popped me with a towel on the backside and laughed.

Miss Carrie was in the sitting room by the fire as it was an unusually cold day for south Arkansas.

"Come in Master Ben," she said. "You look half frozen, boy. Back up to the fire and warm yourself."

We passed the time with small talk mostly about the war. Finally I said, "Miss Carrie, I heard your name was really Carlotta. Is that right?"

"Who told you that, child?"

"My Granny," I replied.

"What else did she tell you?"

"She said the ghost of that Fabre man lived here, too. She said I should stay away from here."

"How did all that come up, Ben? Did you tell her you visit me?"

"Oh, no ma'am. You said that's our secret. I just asked her who lived in this old rundown house. She would faint if she saw the inside of it."

Miss Carrie laughed. "Well, I'll tell you Master Ben. My name is Carlotta Louise Stephens. One of my grandmothers was named Carlotta and the other one was named Louise. My father called me Carlotta, but I didn't like that name. When he died I told Lounicey and her husband, Marshal, to call me Carrie. I wonder how Narcie knew what my name was."

Narcie again. I wondered how she knew Granny was called Narcie, but I didn't ask.

The next few weeks found everyone in Fabre's Bluff on edge. War news was gloomy and frightening. My father and the guard unit were on standby, but by February orders had not come through. I tried not to think about it, but I knew he would have to go and fight. He had said as much.

I visited Miss Carrie often during that time, and she assured me as best she could. I loved my grandmother and knew she would take care of me, but it just wouldn't be the same without my father there.

Finally Dad got the news that the National Guard unit would be deployed. They were to go to Camp Polk in Louisiana for a period of time prior to going overseas. Dad told us they would probably go overseas to fight the Germans since the Navy and Marines were fighting the Japs. How I hated Hitler and Tojo!

I could not sleep the night before Dad was to leave. He looked in on me often, but each time I pretended to be asleep because I didn't want him to worry about me. But I was afraid, very afraid, that he would be killed, and I would be an orphan.

Before daylight he appeared at the door to my room. "I'm awake, Daddy," I said.

He came into the room, sat on the side of my bed and gave me a long hug. "Son," he said, "I hate to have to leave you. I don't want you to worry about me. I'll take care of myself, and I might not even get in battle. But if I do, I promise to be careful.

"I don't worry about you though, because I know you're tough. You'll need to be strong though and help Granny. She'll need you to help her a lot. I know I can depend on you. You are a good boy and old for your years. Almost ten. I'll think of you on your birthday, June twenty-second."

He hugged me again and got up to leave. I said, "I love you, Daddy."

"I love you too, Big Ben," and he left. I hoped he didn't see I was crying as he left.

The next few days were hard for us. Granny tried to keep my spirits up, and I tried to cheer her up, but neither of us was very successful.

I visited Miss Carrie daily during that time, always going through the woods and through her back door. By then she had given me my own key, and that made me feel quite grown-up, because none of my friends had a key to anything. There wasn't even a key to Granny's house.

Saturdays were spent with my friends just messing around as we called it. Most Saturday afternoons were spent at the movies watching Roy Rogers, Gene Autry or many other stars of the era.

One Saturday after the show I could hardly wait to tell Miss Carrie about the movie. I ran through the woods, entered the back door and found her in the sitting room.

"Miss Carrie," I almost yelled, "I've got to tell you something funny."

"Well, sit down and catch your breath and tell me," she said.

"While ago at the show Roy Rogers was in a gunfight. A crook was slipping up behind him fixing to shoot him in the back. Right then a man hollered out, 'Watch out Roy! That blankety-blank is gonna shoot you in the back!' He was really cussing. Every time Roy got in a fight or some kind of jam that man would holler out a warning. We got to laughing and watching him more than the show.

"When the show was over we followed the man out. He was wearing cowboy clothes, a cowboy hat and boots. He had a toy two gun and a holster strapped on.

"He got on a bicycle and turned and rode into the street and a car hit him. It knocked him down and ran over his bicycle. He got up and used his hat to brush himself off.

"A man ran out to him and asked him if he was okay.

"He said, 'Yeah, I'm okay but they killed old Trigger'. Trigger is Roy Rogers' horse, and the man was calling his bicycle Trigger."

I was laughing, but Miss Carrie wasn't. She said, "Ben, that poor man was touched in the head. He was sick. That wasn't funny. It wasn't nice for you to laugh at him. I'm ashamed of you."

She said no more about it nor did I, but I learned a lesson that day.

As the months passed we didn't worry about the war much. Those of us whose fathers were overseas were concerned, but we figured our dads could whip Hitler without much trouble.

Frequent letters from my father came to Granny and me, and they were always uplifting and encouraging. They never said where he was or what he was doing, but we knew he was overseas.

I always felt better after getting his letters, and Granny did too, but most of the time she was just gloomy. She was no fun to be around so I spent more and more time at Miss Carrie's.

I spent less time with my friends, but when we were together we played games related to the war. Our favorite game we called Hitler. We would draw a big circle in the dirt and divide it by drawing a line in the middle. Two boys would play, each standing inside the circle, one on either side of the line. Then each would in turn throw his pocket knife into the ground on his opponent's side of the circle. If the knife stuck in the ground, that boy would draw a line through the cut the knife made to the dividing line and to the edge of the circle. The smaller area would be his property, and we would erase the portion of the original line that remained in his property.

If the other boy's knife didn't stick up in the ground he lost his turn. The game went on until one of the boys had no room left on which to stand. We called it Hitler, because Hitler was dividing up Europe.

My life changed drastically in July of 1944. I was twelve years old.

As I was emerging from the wooded path that led to the back of Miss Carrie's house, Harold rode up on his bicycle.

"What you been doing in those woods?" he asked.

Before I could answer he said, "Your grandmother has been looking all over for you. She sent me to find you. She said if I find you I was to tell you to come home right now. She meant business. You better get on home."

I sat on the cross bars of Harold's bicycle, and he peddled as fast as he could. When we arrived I hopped off and ran to the house. Harold rode off.

When I saw Granny was crying I knew what she was going to tell me.

"Sit down by me, Ben," she said.

I did as she said, and she put her arm around me.

"Honey, I don't know how else to tell you this, so I'll just blurt it out. Your Daddy is dead."

"No!" I screamed.

"Benny, it's true."

"They made a mistake," I cried. "It had to be someone else."

"No, honey, it's true. A young lieutenant came here to tell me. He brought me his things. He was killed on D-Day when they invaded Normandy in France. The lieutenant said he died instantly and didn't suffer at all. In his things was a letter to you."

She handed me a letter in an envelope with my name on it. I didn't want to read it, but I knew I would. I just had to be alone. I couldn't stop crying.

Granny held me in her arms trying to comfort me, but she was crying too. After awhile we composed ourselves and I said, "Granny, will you be okay if I go off by myself to read my letter?"

"Of course, honey, you do as you feel the need. I'll be okay."

I went outside, got on my bike and rode to the wooded path. I rode the bike until the path narrowed and then, leaving the bicycle, I left the path and walked through the thick woods to the river bank.

Sitting on a log I just looked at the envelope for the longest while listening to the birds singing and squirrels barking. Occasionally a fish would jump, making a splash that sounded to me like gunfire.

Finally I opened the envelope and carefully removed the letter, unfolded it and began reading:

"Ben, my son:

"By reading this you know I have been killed in battle. I know you are sad- maybe even crying. That's okay. I want you to know that I did my duty without fear of death. I just hate to leave you.

"We are about to go on a very dangerous mission, and many of us will die. But we won't die for nothing – we'll die fighting bravely for our country so that you and other boys will never have to fight evil men.

"You've got to be big and strong now. Granny will need you. I know you're tough, and I know you can do it.

"Always remember your Dad loved you more than anything in the world. I'm proud of you, son. I want you to know that I was thinking of you and loving you to the very end.

"We're ready to load the boats, so I've got to go now. Always remember I love you."

"Daddy"

After reading the letter I felt the very strong urge to see Miss Carrie. I left my bike and walked the path to her house and climbed the steps onto the porch. Instead of letting myself in I knocked.

Lounicey opened the door, and when she saw I was crying she said, "Oh no, oh dear God in Heaven, no," and she put her hand over her mouth.

Miss Carrie heard Lounicey and came rushing to the door. Saying nothing, she took me in her arms, held me tightly and cried with me.

We went into the sitting room and sat side by side on

the couch.

Finally I said, "Miss Carrie, I'm an orphan now. I killed my mother, and Hitler killed Daddy. God must hate me," and I sobbed violently.

Miss Carrie took me by the shoulders and turned me so that we were sitting face to face.

"Child," she said, "Hitler, or rather his men, did kill your father, but why in the world would you think you killed your mother?"

"By being born," I said. "If I hadn't been born, she would still be alive, and now Daddy's gone too."

Softly but firmly she said, "Ben, you were created out of the love your mother and father had for each other. Your mother died as a complication of the birth, but it wasn't your fault. They wanted a baby, and they knew there were dangers. But they wanted you so bad they created you out of that love. Be proud of that, because you know you were loved."

That was the only time I ever revealed to anyone the guilt I felt about my mother's death.

"I'm going to tell you a story, child. When I was eighteen I was going to be married. His name was Floyd, and he lived in Old Washington over by Hope. He loved me so much, and I loved him so much that we couldn't wait to be married. When the time came he hooked up two horses to his wagon and ran them too hard. Something spooked them, and they ran away. There was a crash, and my Floyd was killed.

"I blamed myself for his death. If I hadn't been in such a hurry he wouldn't have had a runaway and been killed. I was so sad and full of grief and guilt that I fainted and had to take to my bed. All my hair fell out, and when it came back in it was snow white like it is now.

"That's why I became a hermit. But finally I began
to realize that Floyd died not because I loved him but
because he loved me. He was as anxious to marry me as I
was anxious to marry him."

She had tears in her eyes, and for the first time I was
beginning to understand why she was the way she was. I
also began to realize that she really loved me.

Days, weeks and months passed; and I got better but
Granny did not. She cried a lot and kept to herself. Much
of the time she was cross and fussed at me about the most
trivial things.

Rarely she cooked and hardly ate at all. I lived on
baloney and cheese sandwiches when we could get them
to due to rationing. Frequently I had only mustard or
mayonnaise sandwiches. For breakfast it was only cereal.

I spent more and more time at Miss Carrie's. Lounicey
and Marshal had a Victory garden so they had vegetables,
and Miss Carrie insisted I eat with them every day or
two. I would eat whatever I could scrape up at home and
then hurry to Miss Carrie's for a good meal. Granny never
noticed how little I ate, and she ate even less.

My friends began to avoid me. It seemed like I made
them uncomfortable because my father was dead and
theirs weren't. I was an orphan, and they were not. It
seemed to me that they thought hanging around with me
would put a jinx on their fathers and get them killed just
as mine was. That made me sad, but it also made it easier
for me to get to Miss Carrie's.

I was twelve years old when my father was killed and went into the seventh grade that September. Lonnie Joe, Harold, Jody and other boys would play with me at recess, but things were different between us.

My life changed again that September because a new girl was in my class, and she was the most beautiful girl I had ever seen. Her name was Amy. She was almost as tall as I, had light brown hair and dark brown eyes. She had an engaging smile, and I could hardly keep from staring at her.

Toward the end of the first week of school I gathered up my courage and approached her at the end of the day.

"Hi," I said, "my name is Ben Williams. Could I walk with you for awhile?"

"Sure, Ben, my name is Amy McDonald. I'm new. We just moved to Fabre's Bluff. Have you lived here always?"

"Yeah, I was born here. Where did you move here from?"

"We lived all around. My daddy is in the Army. We were living in Fort Knox in Tennessee where Daddy was an instructor teaching soldiers how to drive tanks. He got ordered overseas to command a tank battalion from General Patton. He's somewhere in France now.

"Mama and I moved here to live near my grandparents. After the war is over and Daddy gets out, we're going to move to Little Rock. What about your parents?"

"They're both dead. Mama died when I was born, and Daddy died on D-Day."

"Oh, I'm sorry," she said, and tears came to her eyes. "I worry that my daddy will get killed."

"I'll bet he'll be fine. If he's with General Patton he'll be okay. They'll whip the Germans good. General Patton's the best general in the whole war."

"Here's where I live," she said.

I looked up and was surprised to see Amy lived just three blocks from Miss Carrie.

That night after a meal of fried baloney and an egg I went to Miss Carrie's. I was excited, and Miss Carrie noticed it immediately.

"I am delighted to see you cheerful, Master Ben," she said. "It's been a long time."

"Miss Carrie, I met the nicest girl. She's new in town. Her name is Amy and she lives just down the street from you."

"I know," she said, "she must be Tom and Janet Reynolds's granddaughter. Lounicey told me their daughter and grandchild had moved here to be near them. They live in Hampton."

Miss Carrie smiled and got a twinkle in her eye and said, "But Ben, I didn't think you liked girls."

"I like this one," I exclaimed.

That made her laugh, and she pulled me to her and gave me a big hug.

"I'll tell you what, Ben. If you and Amy become good friends, you can tell her about me and bring her over to see me. But no one else, you understand."

"Yes ma'am," I almost shouted.

The next day was Friday, and I couldn't wait to get to school. Granny wouldn't get out of bed, so I had a bowl of dry cereal for breakfast and left.

My first period class was study hall, and it was also Amy's. I chose a seat by her and whispered, "Amy."

She looked my way and placed her forefinger by her lips indicating I should be quiet. I slipped her a note asking her to go to the movie with me that night. She nodded affirmatively, and I passed another note to her saying I would be by her house about six-thirty to walk to the show. Again she nodded yes.

That school day seemed like a week to me. I saw no more of Amy that day, not even during lunch since fourth period was her lunch time, and fifth period was mine.

After school I saw her standing around talking with some girls. I hoped she was waiting for me.

"Hi, Ben," she said as I walked up. "I thought you would never get here." The other girls giggled, and that made me blush.

I took her book satchel and draped it over my shoulder, and we began to walk without speaking.

Finally I said, "Amy, I really like you. Will you be my girlfriend?"

She looked surprised and then finally said, "I guess so."

That afternoon Granny was still in her nightgown when I got home.

"Ben", she said, "I guess you're going to the show tonight."

"Yes ma'am."

"Well, here's a dollar. Get yourself a hamburger and soda at Snappy Service before the show. The change will get you in the show and buy you some popcorn."

I didn't want to remind her that being twelve I could no longer get in for half price. I now had to pay full price of thirty-five cents. I wanted to pay Amy's way so I would not be able to buy a hamburger if I wanted to buy two dime bags of popcorn at the show.

At about six fifteen I knocked on Amy's door. She came to the door with a nice looking lady.

"Ben, this is my mom," she said.

"Hi, Mrs. McDonald. I'm glad to meet you," I stammered.

Mrs. McDonald laughed and said, "Hello Ben. Don't be nervous. I don't bite."

I didn't know what to say, I was so nervous. But the smile on her face let me know she was teasing.

"What's on at the movies, Ben?" Mrs. McDonald asked.

"It's a double feature, some cowboy show, and then I think it's a Boston Blackie movie. There'll be a newsreel and a cartoon. The show ought to be over by nine or nine-fifteen."

"Well, you kids have a good time and come straight home after the show."

We only had about eight blocks to walk. We talked about school and Amy's new friends on the way.

While watching the movie Amy let me hold her hand – something I had never done with any girl. The cowboy show was first and then a cartoon followed by Boston Blackie. We got in after the news which was just as well for I feared news of the war would be disturbing.

In the middle of the Boston Blackie show, after about the third murder, Amy said, "I don't like this show. Can we leave?"

I said, "Sure," and we excused ourselves and walked out.

Outside, as we walked, Amy said, "I'm sorry Ben, but I just don't like all that killing."

She started to cry.

"I know, Amy, but it's just a movie. They really weren't killed."

"Of course they weren't. I know that. It just scares me, because I'm afraid Daddy will get killed."

"My Daddy was killed," I said, "but that doesn't mean yours will. He'll be in a tank. That's a lot of protection. Besides, General Patton won't let anything happen to him."

"I hope not," she replied. "I pray for him every night."

She stopped crying and I said, "Listen, Amy, I've got a surprise for you. Tomorrow I want you to meet someone – a real nice old lady. But you'll have to cross your heart and hope to die that you won't tell anyone, not even your mother, about her."

"I don't know about that, Ben."

"I promise, she's real nice. She's just real shy. She told me I could bring you by but nobody else. I just love her. I know you'll like her."

"Okay, but who is she and where does she live?" Amy said a little fearfully.

"Not far from you, but remember you can't tell anyone or else you can't go."

"Okay, I cross my heart and hope to die I won't tell."

I wanted to kiss her goodnight, but I thought I'd better not press my luck. I just told her I had a good time and that I would come by about ten the next morning.

I could hardly sleep that night. I tossed and turned and had weird dreams. Finally morning came. Granny was up for a change and fixed me some hot oatmeal for breakfast. She had little to say, though, and didn't ask me where I was going as I left.

At a quarter to ten I knocked at Amy's door. She came out dressed in a short sleeve shirt, shorts, and sandals.

I said, "Amy, you better go back in and put on blue jeans and tennis shoes. We're gonna be walking down a path through some woods."

She looked a little frightened and asked, "Where are you taking me, Ben?"

"It's nothing to be afraid of, I promise."

She went back inside, and in a few minutes came back out wearing jeans, tennis shoes and a long-sleeved shirt.

We walked through the woods to the hidden path along the bluff bank of the Ouachita River. I was aware of Amy's cautiousness. I assured her it would be okay.

As we entered the clearing behind the house, Amy's eyes got big and she said, "Oh no, Ben. That's the crazy woman's house." She became agitated and said, "I can't believe you brought me here. What are you trying to do?"

"Trust me, Amy, you're gonna get the surprise of your life. You're about to meet the nicest lady you ever saw. But remember, you can tell no one."

We approached the kitchen door, and I took the key from my pocket and unlocked the door.

As we entered, Amy had a very surprised look and said, "I can't believe it. This house is really nice on the inside."

"I know," I replied.

Miss Carrie entered the room and said, "Dear Ben, hello. And this is Amy. What a beautiful young girl. I am so glad to meet you, Amy. I knew my Ben was sweet on you." I blushed, Amy smiled and Miss Carrie winked at us.

"Come into the sitting room," she said as Lounicey entered. "This is Lounicey. She is my dear friend and the lady who keeps house for me."

"How do, Miss Amy," said Lounicey. "Master Ben, you sho' do know how to pick 'em."

Miss Carrie laughed and Amy and I blushed. We entered the sitting room, and Miss Carrie motioned for Amy and me to sit on the couch. Miss Carrie sat in the fireside easy chair.

"Amy, I'll bet you thought Ben was bringing you to an old haunted house, didn't you?"

Amy had relaxed and was taking in the beauty of the room. "I didn't know what to think. I didn't expect this. This is a mansion."

Miss Carrie laughed and said, "No, child, this isn't a mansion. It's just an old woman's home – an old woman who long ago abandoned the outside world. I love my pretty things and especially my books. Do you like to read?"

"Oh, yes ma'am, especially poetry."

"I'll tell you what," Miss Carrie said, "I have many books of poetry. You can come here any time you want and read poetry. Have you ever read Evangeline?"

"No ma'am."

She went to the bookcase and picked a book from off the shelf.

"This book is about one hundred years old. It was published in eighteen hundred and forty six - ninety eight years ago. I want you to come here to read it. It is the story of a young woman, Evangeline, who searches the world over for her lover, Gabriel. It has the most beautiful first line of any poem I have ever read. It starts, 'This is the forest primeval.' Isn't that lovely? That's all I'm going to tell you, but I want you to read it. Will you?"

"Oh, yes ma'am."

"Good! I will say this. It is a story of searching. I searched and almost found. Young Ben is searching; he just doesn't know it. I hope he finds what he is looking for. Who knows, it may be you."

Amy and I looked at each other. Neither of us knew what she was talking about.

Miss Carrie took the book and placed it back on the shelf.

"Amy," she said, "come anytime you like. You don't need to knock, and Ben will show you where the key is hidden. You don't have to come with Ben but can come alone if you like. But always come by way of the path you and Ben took today. And please tell no one, not even your mother or your grandparents. Humor this old woman and help me maintain my privacy."

"I promise, Miss Carrie. I'll tell no one, and I will come

back. I love it here."

I saw a tear in Miss Carrie's eye.

Just then Lounicey came in with hot chocolate and a pie. She cut the pie in quarters – a large piece for each of us. She scooped whipped cream on top of each piece, and we all four sat down and ate.

"Lounicey," Amy exclaimed, "this is the best pie I ever ate. What kind is it?"

"Sweet potato," Lounicey replied.

"It is Lounicey's world famous sweet potato pie, only the world doesn't know it. Only she and I and Marshal eat it."

When we were walking home Amy said, "Ben, I will never forget this day. It is the happiest day I have ever had. Miss Carrie is wonderful. Thank you for bringing me."

"I love her," was all I could say. I did love her, and I was in awe of her. There was a mystery about her that bewildered me. Why did she care for me so much? Why was she so nice to Amy when she didn't even know her? Why had she isolated herself from the world? And most of all, why had she allowed me, and now Amy, in?

As time went by Amy and I were together almost daily. Sometime we went to Miss Carrie's together, and sometimes each of us went alone.

Amy began reading Evangeline and told me it was the saddest poem she had ever read.

Thanksgiving we had a late afternoon traditional

meal with Miss Carrie. It was Amy's second meal and my first, since Granny was more morose that day than usual. On Monday after Thanksgiving I got dressed for school. There was no sound from Granny's room, and her door was closed. I had a glass of milk and left for school.

Most of the day I worried about Granny and was unable to concentrate on school work. Finally the three-thirty bell rang, and I rushed out, not even looking for Amy.

When I got home I found Granny's door still closed, and she was nowhere to be seen. I knocked on her door several times but got no answer. Finally I opened the door and entered her room.

Granny looked very pale, almost blue, and lay motionless in the bed. When I shook her to awaken her she was very cold. I was afraid she was dead.

I ran to the phone and lifted it off its cradle. When the operator said, "Number please," I said, "Please help me. I'm Ben. I think my grandmother's dead."

"Stay right there, Ben, I'll send someone to help you," she said.

I went into the kitchen to wait. I just couldn't go into the bedroom where she was. In what seemed like hours, but was only a few minutes, a policeman and an ambulance came.

The policeman and the two men from the ambulance went into Granny's room. When they came out the policeman said, "Son, you were right. Your grandmother has passed away." I cried, and he took me in his arms and hugged me.

The ambulance men told me they worked at the funeral home and would take Granny there. The policeman stayed with me and made a call on the phone.

I overheard him say, "Pearl, Miz Guillaume has expired. Young Ben is all alone. Can you come over right now?"

He paused, then hung up the phone and came back into the living room. "Ben," he said, "a nice lady is going to be here in a minute to take care of you. I'll wait here with you until she arrives."

I said nothing but just sat there beside him. Now I was really an orphan.

After a short time a middle aged fat lady came in without knocking. She looked at the policeman and said, "You can leave now, George, I'll take over."

He hugged me again and then left.

The lady said, "I'm Miz Pearl Greene, Ben. I'm going to take care of you. I work for the state's child welfare service. We've been concerned about you for some time considering you being an orphan and all and your grandmother not doing too well."

I said, "We've been doing fine."

She said, "I know better, Ben. We've got a plan for you, and we should have done it before now. Come on into your room. We need to pack your clothes in a suitcase."

"I don't want to leave here," I almost shouted...

"But you've got to, son; you have no one to care for you now."

"Yes I do; I know someone I can live with," I replied.

"Who is that?" she asked.

"I can't tell you," I said, "but if you let me go see her I know she'll say okay."

"Well then, let's go see her."

"You can't go. I have to go by myself."

Miss Pearl looked at me with a frown on her face. I thought she was about to get mad. I was very afraid so I said no more.

She took me into my room and packed all the clothes into a suitcase. She said, "Come on," and took my by the hand and led me to her car.

"Where are you taking me?" I cried.

"To the orphanage in Little Rock," she said.

"No," I shouted, "I don't want to go!"

"You have no choice," she said. "You have no one to live with, and you're too young to live alone."

Now I was really alone. I couldn't go see Miss Carrie, and I couldn't even call Amy. All I could do was get in the car with a woman who didn't care for me at all, only about doing her job.

In the car I asked the lady, "What about my grandmother? Will she get a funeral?"

"She has burial insurance. They told me that at the funeral home. They'll give her a small service at the cemetery."

"Why can't I go to it?" I asked.

"Because you'll be at the orphanage, that's why. Now be quiet so I can drive and not be distracted."

"That's not fair," I said. "I ought to be able to go to her funeral. There's people I need to call. You didn't even let me do that!"

"Boy," she said, "you are only twelve years old. Someone's got to take care of you. You don't have any kinfolks, so I've got to take you to the orphanage. So just shut up and let me do my job."

I decided there was nothing I could do. I just wished that woman would drop dead and leave me alone. I had no idea what the orphanage would be like, but I had heard jokes and other stories about them. Nothing I had heard had ever sounded pleasant.

When I cried along the way I tried to be quiet. I didn't want to make the woman any madder than she already seemed. I vowed to myself, however, that somehow, some way, I would get back to Fabre's Bluff and see Miss Carrie and Amy again.

It was dark by the time we reached the orphanage. Miss Pearl took my suitcase in one hand and my hand in the other and almost dragged me up the front steps. Almost immediately the door was opened by a pleasant looking middle aged lady.

"Hi, Ben," the lady said. "I am Miss Claudia. I'm the evening supervisor, and I hope to be your friend."

She smiled and I felt a little at ease. She seemed to be a nice lady. She took my bag and led me down the hall, which was long and dark and narrow. On either side of the hall were doors leading to what I assumed to be offices. At the end of the hall was a wide staircase. Miss Pearl left as soon as Miss Claudia took my bag.

As we walked Miss Claudia said, "Now Ben, we have

rules that all our residents must follow. The second floor is the girls' floor, and the third is for the boys. There will be no girls ever to be on the third floor and no boys on the second.

"Boys and girls are to sit at separate tables in the dining room. You may play together on the playground, but nowhere else. While on the playground you are to remain in sight of the playground supervisor at all times. You will be in a room with two other boys, Randall and Samuel. They are your age and are very nice boys.

"Wake up time is six-thirty, lunch is at noon and dinner is at six. You will be enrolled at local schools, and we will take you there and pick you up.

"You will have certain chores that we will talk about later. This is to be your home until you are eighteen. We hope you will like it here."

Some home, I thought.

The walk up the stairs seemed to take forever. My thoughts were on escaping and getting back to Fabre's Bluff. I felt if I could just get back there Miss Carrie would take care of me, maybe even let me live with her. I couldn't let myself think of where I would live if Miss Carrie wouldn't take me in.

The third floor hall extended the entire length of the building and was lined by a row of closed doors on either side. The third door on the left was to be my room.

Miss Claudia knocked and then opened the door without waiting for a response. There were three narrow beds in the room, two of which were stacked as bunk beds. There were three small desks, each with a ladder-back chair. In the outside wall of the room was a window. I noticed that the window was covered on the outside by a heavy wire screen.

One boy was lying on the top bunk reading and another was sitting at a desk.

Miss Claudia said, "Boys, this is Ben. He will be living with you." She nodded toward the boy on the top bunk and said, "Ben, that is Randall, and he is Samuel. Boys, say hello to Ben."

"Hi," said Samuel. Randall just nodded.

After she left Samuel said, "Call me Sammy, and he's Randy. You can have the bottom drawer of the chest and the back rod in the closet. Take the bottom bunk. Randy likes the top, and I've got the single bed. That's your desk," as he nodded to the desk below the window.

I tried to say hi but started to cry. Randy jumped down and said, "It's okay, Ben, everybody cries when he first gets here, but it's really not too bad a place. They treat you okay if you don't screw up. If you do, they'll send you to Mr. Baker, the head guy. If you have to go see him you're in big trouble."

I unpacked my few belongings and hung my coat in the closet. "Where's the bathroom? I've gotta go take a leak," I said.

"Down the hall, last door on the left," said Sammy. "There's six johns, and all of 'em are open. When several guys are taking a dump at the same time it gets pretty rank in there. Smells like a skunk convention." Randy laughed.

I found the bathroom, and Sammy was right. There were six commodes in a row on one wall and six lavatories on the opposite wall. At the far end of the room was an open area with six shower heads. I figured there must be fifteen or twenty boys on the floor, so it was liable to be very congested each morning. I decided I would just get up earlier than the others and get there first each day.

When I got back to the room we all got in our pajamas and went to bed. They told me that lights out was at nine, so we just lay there in the dark.

"I'm gonna find a way to slip out of this place and go home. Have y'all ever tried it?" I asked.

Randy said, "Ain't no use tryin'. There's that wire on all the windows, and anyway we're up three stories. Ain't no way to get down even if you got out."

Sammy added, "Ben, we're twelve years old. We don't have anybody; we're orphans. Where would we go and how would we live? Besides, it's not bad here. Almost everybody is nice."

"Well, if I can get out of here I'll go back to the Bluff. There's a lady there who'll take care of me," I said.

"Bullshit," said Randy.

We got quiet and soon the others were asleep. I lay there thinking of ways to escape and get home until I fell asleep.

Time passed slowly at the orphanage. Occasionally a younger child would be adopted, but I never knew of anyone over three being adopted. Babies were kept in another building, so I never knew about them.

The food was not bad. In fact, most of the time it was

real good. If you missed a meal, though, it was just tough. There were no between meal snacks.

I was enrolled in the seventh grade at East Side Junior High, the same school my roommates attended. It wasn't a bad school, but wasn't as nice as the school in Fabre's Bluff. Most of the kids were from the wrong side of the tracks and some were tough and were always looking for a fight.

One day Joe Bob, a bully, pushed me too far, and we got into a fight. I was holding my own and got in a lucky punch that bloodied his nose just as the principal broke us up and took us to his office.

"You boys will have to stay after school for the rest of the week," he said.

"I can't do that, Mr. Purifoy," I said. "I'll miss my ride home." I didn't want Joe Bob to know I was an orphan and lived at the orphanage, so I said no more.

Mr. Purifoy, of course, knew and must have understood why I said home instead of orphanage. "Okay, boys," he said, "I'm going to let you off this time. Go back to class and behave yourselves."

After that I had no more trouble with the bullies, and Joe Bob and I actually became friends.

The third Saturday I was in the orphanage I was called away from the table at lunch by Mr. Baker, the superintendent. "Ben," he said, "come with me. There is someone in the office who wants to see you."

I grabbed one last bite and got up to follow Mr. Baker

out of the lunchroom and down the hall. I wondered who
could be coming to see me. I hadn't been in trouble at
school or in the orphanage. I was very concerned if not
actually afraid.

"Who is it, Mr. Baker? Who wants to see me? Am I in
trouble?"

"You're not in any trouble, Ben," he replied. "It's a man
from Fabre's Bluff."

That caused a burst of excitement which I tried not
to show. Maybe it was someone to get me out of the
orphanage and back to Fabre's Bluff.

Mr. Baker opened the door to the reception room and
led me through and into his private office. Sitting on a
couch was a rather portly and baldheaded man dressed
in a dark blue suit with a red necktie. I noticed he had on
wing-tipped shoes.

"Ben, this is Mr. Phillips. I'll leave you two to talk,"
said Mr. Baker, as he retreated from the room, closing the
door behind him.

Mr. Phillips motioned for me to sit down beside him. I
did as he suggested.

"Young man," he said, "my name is H. David Phillips.
I'm a lawyer, and I represent Miss Carrie Stephens. I am
here at her request. Let me say that I knew your father
well. He was a fine man, and if you grow to be half the
man he was you will go far in life.

"Miss Carrie has told me all about you. She has really
taken a liking to you. She would like for you to be able to
get out of here and come live with her."

I almost shouted with joy.

"Now hold your horses, young man. You know how
Miss Carrie is. She can't get out of her house, and people
are scared of her so it'll take some doing on my part. I

don't even know if it can be worked out, but I'm going to try my best. Miss Carrie wanted me to tell you to be a good boy and be patient."

I said nothing but just sat there looking away from him and toward the window hoping Mr. Phillips could not see my face if I started to cry. I didn't cry, though; because I knew I was stuck here. I knew they wouldn't let me live with an old hermit lady. They just didn't know how really nice she was.

Mr. Phillips stood up and straightened his coat. I noticed he pulled at the seat of his pants to get it unstuck from his bottom. As we parted, and I watched him walk out to his car, I never felt more alone in all my life.

Weeks passed, and nothing happened. I decided that Mr. Phillips had failed and that I was stuck here until I was grown. I didn't blame Miss Carrie. I knew she couldn't get out and around. I just wished people knew her as I did.

Christmas came and passed. The orphanage staff tried to make the season festive and fun, and they were fairly successful. But being in an institution is just not in any way like being in your own home with people who love you.

I had memories of my dad and me going into the woods in his pick-up truck. He would let me pick out the tree I wanted, and he would cut it down. I'd help him load it in the bed of the truck, and he, Granny and I would decorate it while each of us drank a cup of hot cider. Those days were gone forever. I decided if I ever had children I would make Christmas happy and cheerful for them.

I also decided I could not stay here. No one mistreated me. Quite the contrary, everyone was very nice to me. But however hard I tried, I could not make this place feel like home. I vowed to escape however long it took and however difficult it was.

I knew I couldn't just run away from school, because there would be very little time between when I left and when I was missed. I decided the best time would be around ten at night. I would have about eight hours before I was missed. Now all I had to do was find a way to get outside.

The only escape route I felt was through the janitor's closet at the far end of our hall. I had noticed at one time, when the janitor had left the door open for a few minutes, that there was no screen on the window inside that room.

The janitor usually made his rounds about eight o'clock each night. I developed a plan and swore Randy and Sammy to secrecy. They said I was crazy but promised to tell no one.

I chose a Friday night because everyone would sleep late on Saturday. I was late for supper on the appointed night, and while everyone was in the dining room I took my coat and packed suitcase to the bathroom and left them in a dark corner. I then went to the dining room and ate everything on my plate and anything that Sammy and Randy didn't eat.

When we got back to the room I said, "Okay boys, this is it. I'm leaving tonight. Remember, you promised!"

Sammy said, "We won't tell on you, but it's cold out there. You'll freeze to death. How're you gonna get out of here?"

"I've got a plan, but I'm not gonna tell you all. If

you don't know it, nobody can get it out of you."

At a little before eight I told my roommates goodbye
and went into the hall. When I heard the janitor's
footsteps on the stairs I ran my finger down my throat
and gagged myself causing me to vomit on the floor. I then
walked toward the stairs, and when the janitor appeared I
said, "Mr. Johnson, someone threw up all over the floor."

He said, "I'll clean it up. You go to your room."

"I've got to go to the bathroom," I said, and headed
down the hall. Mr. Johnson walked with me as far as the
janitor's closet and unlocked the door.

I went into the bathroom and kept the door barely
cracked. Shortly I saw Mr. Johnson come out of the closet
and walk down the hall, mop and bucket in hand. Sure
enough he left the closet door unlocked.

I grabbed my suitcase and coat and slipped through
the unlocked door into the room. I hid under a large table
in the far end of the room. I could feel my rapid pulse
beating in my neck.

In a few minutes I heard the janitor empty his bucket
in a toilet next door. He flushed the toilet and soon entered
the storeroom. He put down the mop and bucket, turned
out the light and left the room. I heard him lock the door.

After waiting long enough for the janitor to leave the
floor I opened the window and dropped my suitcase and
coat to the ground, taking care to drop them into shrubs
so as not to make too much noise. I jumped three feet to a
large limb of an oak tree and climbed down to the ground,
put on my coat, picked up my suitcase and walked on
down the road.

I was free. Now I had to figure out how to get home.

The night was colder than I thought it would be, and I began to shiver. Had I done the right thing, I thought, or was I a fool? I didn't know, but I knew I had to get warm soon.

Hitchhiking on the road south was not a good idea, because when I was missed the highway would be the first place the police would look. I decided the best choice would be to hop a freight train like I had seen hoboes do in Fabre's Bluff in the late thirties and early forties. So instead of heading south toward the Bluff, I headed north along the tracks to where I figured the classification yard would be.

I ran for a while to keep warm and walked when I got winded or tired. Soon I reached the yard and saw many boxcars, some open and some closed. Some were attached to other cars and an engine, and some were either unattached or attached to other cars but not to an engine.

I decided to climb into a car hooked up to form a train. I found one with one door open and the opposite door closed and the engine pointed to the south. There were some boxes scattered about and straw on the floor. I laid down on straw and pulled some over me for warmth.

Soon I drifted off to sleep and awoke when I felt the train begin to move. Just then someone threw a bundle into the car and then jumped in. I was frightened, but I asked, "Who are you?"

"What!" the man exclaimed. He lit a match and saw me.

"Damn, boy," he said, "you scared the shit out of me.

What are you doin' on this train? You're just a kid."

I saw, when he lit another match, that he was a small colored man dressed in ragged clothes. He needed a shave. I hoped he was not mean. I decided to take my chances and tell him the truth and hope he would help me.

"I'm twelve and a half, and I'm an orphan. I'm running away from the orphanage and going to Fabre's Bluff. That's where I used to live. I don't want to live in an orphanage."

"I don't blame you none," he said. "I guess you might say I'm a grown up orphan, 'cause I ain't got no kin at all – not one person in the whole damn world. You goin' the right direction, boy, but the closest you gonna get to Fabre's Bluff is about forty miles if you get off'n the train at Gurdon and about the same if you get off at Prescott. If you get off at Hope you got about fifty miles. You best hope the train slows enough to jump off in Gurdon or Prescott, else you got ten more miles to go from Hope. If it don't slow at none of them places you out of luck 'cause it'll be Texarkana 'fore you can get off. In that case, you liable never to get to home."

"Can you help me, mister? I don't know anything about being a hobo."

He laughed and said that he would help me.

"What's your name, boy?" he asked.

"Ben," I replied. "What's yours?"

"Little Sam," he said. "I used to run with Big Sam, but he got killed when he tried to jump a train, and the train run over him. Now don't you jump off'n this train lessin' I tells you, you hear me?"

"Yes sir," I said, "I'll do what you say."

He sat down beside me and moved real close. "You freezin' to death, boy. Scoot up close to me, and I'll keep you warm. You want somethin' to eat?"

"No sir, I had a big supper."

I moved close to him, and the heat of his body and the pile of straw warmed me. The warmth of his body and the clackety-clack of the wheels on the rails soon lulled me to sleep.

It was still dark when Sam gently shook me awake. He said, "We's goin' through Gurdon, and we slow enough for you to jump. You better jump now, Ben, 'cause you may not get another chance. Throw your suitcase first and then jump."

I threw my suitcase out and as I jumped I heard him yell, "Good luck and God be with you."

I wandered the dark streets until dawn. The early morning light was such that I was able to get my bearings. I knew I must go south and east. I knew which way was south, because the train had been going south. By facing south I knew that east would be to my left. The rising sun confirmed that opinion.

I wandered eastward on what looked to be the main street of the town. Before I went far I saw a police car. I hoped the driver of the car hadn't seen me and tried to slip into an alley, but it was too late.

The car pulled up beside me, and a fat policeman emerged and approached me. I noticed his big sidearm and was impressed that his belly overlapped his belt making it impossible to see his belt buckle.

"Awful early for you to be out, ain't it son? You got a

grip there. You ain't runnin' away from home, are you?"

"No sir," I said, rather emphatically.

"Well what you doin' with that grip then?" he asked.

"I'm going home to Fabre's Bluff," I replied.

"What you doin' in Gurdon at the crack of dawn with no adults around?"

"I was in North Little Rock," I lied, "and I didn't have the money for a bus ticket, so I went to the train yard and asked a man if I could ride with him in the caboose. He said I could. This was the closest place to the Bluff I could get so I got off here to hitchhike home."

"I didn't hear no train stop," he said.

"It didn't, but it slowed down enough for me to jump. The man said it wouldn't stop until Texarkana so I'd better get off here where it was closer. So I threw my bag off and jumped. It was going real slow."

"I don't know whether I believe you or not," he said.

"It's the truth, I swear," I said.

"Who you goin' to see in Fabre's Bluff?" he asked.

The look on his face made me think he was trying to believe me.

"Mister," I said, "I'll tell you the truth. I was living in North Little Rock with my stepmother while my daddy was off to war. She was mean to me. My daddy got killed, and she even got meaner. She told me she wished she'd never seen me. So I did run away, but I'm going to live with my grandmother in Fabre's Bluff."

"What's your grandmother's name?" he asked.

"Narcissa Guillaume," I replied.

"I think I heard tell of her. Okay, boy," he said. "You go on down this street and take a right down yonder where it turns. If you don't catch a ride in a little bit, there'll be a colored man come by in a wagon pulled by two mules

after awhile. I'll tell him to look out for you and give you a
ride. He'll be goin' to Chidester, but that'll get you within
thirteen miles of the Bluff. You can walk that far if you
have to. Now go ahead and get gone."

I didn't hesitate. I thanked him and took off, much
relieved that I was still free.

As I walked through Gurdon I noticed people going to
their outhouses and some emptying the contents of slop
jars into the roadside ditches. No one paid any attention to
me.

By the time the sun was well up I had reached the edge
of town. I decided it would be best to wait for the man in
the wagon, because people in cars might have heard of a
runaway from the orphanage. I realized that was unlikely
since it was so early in the day, but I wanted to take no
chances. Whenever I heard or saw a car or truck coming I
left the road and hid in the bushes.

Finally after I had walked about a mile out of town I
saw a mule-drawn wagon approach. I emerged from the
bushes and waved. An elderly Negro man waved back.

The wagon stopped, and I approached it. "You gotta be
Ben," the man said. "Jump up in the wagon and sit down
beside me. I be Clell Eaves. You goin' to the Bluff I hear.
You's a runaway so when you see some'un a'comin' you
jump up in under the seat. No need to take no chances on
getting' caught. I sho' don't wanna get in no trouble for
carryin' off no runaway."

"Thanks, Mister Clell," I said, as I climbed in.

"You don't have to mister me, boy. I'm just a old colored man what's mindin' my own business most of the time, but the policeman asked me to help you so that's what I'm a'doin'. Who you goin' to see?"

"Miss Carrie Stephens."

"I don't know her," he replied.

"Do you know Lounicey and Marshal? They work for her."

"You mean Sweet Pea? Hell, yes I knows 'em. They works for that old witch woman. What's you goin' to see that old woman for?" he asked as he took off his hat and scratched his head.

"She's not a witch. She's a nice old lady that just wants to be left alone. She just wants people to think she's mean and lives in a haunted house so they won't bother her," I replied.

"Well I be doggone," he said. "I always wondered why Sweet Pea worked for that old woman. I guess now I knows."

The trip to Chidester took well over two hours, and when we arrived at the edge of town, Clell turned and noticed one of the mules was moving his bowels. He pulled up, stopped and handed me the reins. "Hold tight Ben," he said. "I gotta go pick up them road apples. I don't want the town marshal to get onto me."

Soon we arrived at the Chidester Mercantile and said our goodbyes. I started afoot to Fabre's Bluff.

As I walked along the gravel road from Chidester to

Fabre's Bluff the sun felt good on my face but warmed me only slightly. It was very cold, and the moisture from my breath made it appear I was smoking.

There was little or no traffic on the road. I was glad of that since I would not have to hide or explain why I was afoot.

After about an hour a man came by on horseback. He stopped and said, "Boy, what you doin' out awalkin' on a cold day like this? Where you headed?"

"I'm going to the Bluff," I replied.

"Damn, boy, that's another ten miles. I'm goin' to the Maul community. Hop on and you can ride that far. That'll leave you only a mile or two to walk," he said.

He took his foot out of the left stirrup, held out his left hand and said, "Grab aholt, step in the stirrup and climb on behind. You'll have to hold your bag beside you."

I did as he suggested, straddled the horse behind the rider, wrapped my left arm around his waist and held my suitcase in my right hand.

The ride was rough and more than once I almost fell. Once I dropped the suitcase, and the man let me climb down and get it and then climb back on.

"Who you goin' to see in the Bluff?" he asked.

"My granny," I replied.

"Who's that?"

"Narcie Guillaume," I replied.

"Don't you shit me, boy. She died here while back."

"I'm sorry, mister. I meant to say my other grandmother."

"Well, who's she?" he aside rather sternly.

"Miss Carrie Stephens," I lied.

"Well, I'll be double damned," he said. "I didn't even know that old witch had ever been married and, much less, had kids."

"Well she did," I said.

We rode on in silence and finally he turned off on the
Maul road and said, "Here's where you get off boy. You'll
have to walk the rest of the way. Tell your old witch
granny I said Boo!" and he laughed loudly.

By the sun in the far southwest I guessed it was about
four o'clock when I started walking. I turned to wave to
the rider. He blew his nose on a red bandana and then
waved the bandana at me. I hoped nothing shook off the
bandana onto him, waved again and turned to the south.

It was about two miles to Bluff Street and Miss
Carrie's house. I took the long way there carefully avoiding
the main street hoping to not be noticed. Once I thought
a lady recognized me so I just tucked my head and raised
my free hand to my face as though to scratch my head. The
lady turned away, and I walked on.

I was relieved when I reached the entrance to the
wooded path that led to the back of Miss Carrie's house. I
was excited yet also tired, and I all but ran along the path
until I reached the house. It seemed as though I had been
gone for years rather than just a few months.

As I approached the kitchen door I heard Marshal call
out, "Master Ben!"

Lounicey heard his call, looked out the window and
suddenly was at the door. "Lawdee, Ben, how'd you get
here? Miss Carrie gonna faint when she see you!"

She took me in her arms and gave me a long hug, and I

began to cry.

Miss Carrie came into the kitchen saying, "What's all this --- Ben, dear Ben," she exclaimed. "What in the world are you doing here?"

"I'm not going back, Miss Carrie. I hate it there. I'll live by myself in Granny's house and eat with you sometime if you'll let me. Please, Miss Carrie!" and I began to sob.

She took me in her arms and also began to cry. She gently rubbed the back of my head and said, "Hush, Ben, it's going to be all right. Mr. Phillips, the man who came to see you, he's my lawyer. He's trying to work it out so that you can live with me. He's a good lawyer. He'll be able to get it done. Don't you fret anymore at all. Lounicey, get this hungry boy something to eat."

"Yes ma'am," loudly said the grinning Lounicey.

I was hungry and exhausted, but I felt I was home.

By the time I finished eating it was dark. Miss Carrie told Lounicey she could go home, took me by the hand and said, "Come on, Ben, sit with me by the fire."

We went into the living room and sat side by side on a small couch. For awhile we said nothing but just looked at the flickering flames in the fireplace and enjoyed the warmth.

I was very tired and about to fall asleep when Miss Carrie said, "Dear Ben, you know you must return to the orphanage for a short time don't you?"

That aroused me and I spoke up as she took my hand in hers. I said, "Miss Carrie, I hate that place. Please don't make me go back."

"But, honey, you must. If Mr. Phillips is going to be
successful getting the court to make you my ward, you are
going to have to be in compliance with the court order."

"What does that mean?" I asked.

"It means you have got to mind the judge and do
what he says. If you don't, the judge will declare you a
delinquent, and he will send you back and we will have no
chance of him allowing you to live with me. Honey, I love
you and want you with me always, but we have no choice
in the matter. It will be strictly up to the judge, so we
mustn't make him mad."

Her saying she loved me made me cry, and she thought
it was because I had to go back. She said, "Don't cry, Ben.
We must all do what we have to do, no matter what."

"That's not it, Miss Carrie. I'll do what you tell me to
do. I just don't want to live there till I'm grown."

Miss Carrie had tears in her eyes when she pulled me
to her and hugged me. "Ben," she said ever so softly, "I
promise I'll do whatever it takes to keep you with me. Now
come on and let's get you to bed."

She took me to a bedroom on the second floor, hugged
me again and tucked me in. The weight of the quilts gave
me a secure feeling and a warmth I had not felt for over
twenty-four hours. She kissed me on the cheek, tousled
my hair and said, "Sweet dreams, dear boy. I love you so."

As tired as I was I lay in bed and thought about how
nice it would be if this could be my home. I had never been

upstairs in this house and was fascinated by the view of the reflection of the full moon on the glimmering water of the Ouachita River. I felt as though I were in a fantasy land when I finally fell asleep.

When I awoke the next morning the wind was blowing, and it was snowing heavily. I dressed quickly and went downstairs.

I found Miss Carrie and Mr. Phillips sitting at the kitchen table drinking coffee.

"Sit down with us, Ben," she said. "You remember Mr. Phillips, don't you?"

"Yes ma'am," I replied.

"How are you, son?" asked the lawyer.

"I'm okay," I replied, "but I'll be fine if you can get the judge to let me live with Miss Carrie."

"I'm going to do my best," he replied, "but I don't want you to get your hopes up too high. You are not blood kin to Miss Carrie, and people don't understand that she's not some kind of hermit or witch or something. It's going to be hard but we won't go down without a fight."

Miss Carrie spoke up and said, "Well anyway he can't go back today in this blizzard."

"I know," he replied. "I've already phoned the orphanage and told them he is safe and in my care. They agreed he could stay with me until this is all worked out."

"H. David," Miss Carrie said in a very stern and serious voice," you do whatever it takes, no matter the cost. I want this boy to live with me."

"I'll do my best. That's all I can promise."

"I know you will," she said.

It snowed hard the rest of that Sunday. The wind blew hard and caused snow to pile up in the inner corners of the house. I had never seen that much snow. I sat on the couch by Miss Carrie, and we watched the flickering flames in the fireplace. We said nothing, just sat quietly. The sound of the wind and the warmth of the fire made me drowsy, and Miss Carrie pulled me toward her and laid me down, my head in her lap.

Soon I was asleep. When I awoke it was almost dark, and still I lay where I had fallen asleep with my head in her lap. With one hand she was running her fingers through my hair, and with the other she was gently rubbing my back. Barely awake, I heard her whisper, "Dear Ben, I love you so. I think of you as the son Floyd and I could have had."

When she realized I was awake she said no more. As I aroused and sat up she asked, "Are you hungry, child?"

"Yes ma'am," I replied.

"Well come on with me into the kitchen, and I'll fix us some ham and eggs and biscuits. You'll have to help me, because I sent Lounicey home because of the snow. I declare, in all my seventy-nine years, I don't believe I ever saw it snow this much. Child, if you had been a day late leaving Little Rock, you would have likely frozen to death in this blizzard. Thank God you left when you did."

While Miss Carrie fried a big piece of ham and four eggs she let me knead the dough for the biscuits. When the food was ready we sat down to eat, and Miss Carrie brought a large jar of honey.

As I was spreading butter and honey on my two biscuits she said, "Ben, do you know the only food that never spoils no matter what?"

"No ma'am, I don't."

"It's honey, and it's the only food that never spoils. You don't have to put it in the icebox. You can even leave it out in the open on the table, and it won't spoil. Even a year later it will still be good. And it's good for you too."

I was only twelve years old, but I was amazed at how smart Miss Carrie was and how much I had learned from her.

After we cleaned up following our meal Miss Carrie said, "It's about time for you to go to bed, child. Come on and I'll tuck you in. Let's get you to bed now. You need your sleep. You know a child grows most while he's sleeping."

She took me by the hand and led me up the stairs to the bedroom. I hoped that could be my room always. She told me to get into some bed clothes she laid out for me and use the slop jar. She would wait in the hall until I was through and ready for bed.

When I finished I got in bed, pulled up the cover and called out, "I'm in bed, Miss Carrie."

She came into the room, tucked the cover between the springs and the mattress and said, "It's time for your prayers, Ben."

I said, "Now I lay me down to sleep, I pray thee, Lord, my soul to keep. If I should die before I wake, I pray thee,

Lord, my soul to take. God bless my mother and daddy and granny in heaven. Bless Lounicey and Marshal. And, most of all, bless Miss Carrie and let me live with her forever. And, oh yes, bless Mr. Floyd in heaven. Amen."

She sat on the side of the bed and gently rubbed my head while softly humming a tune unfamiliar to me. My eyelids got very heavy. The last thing I heard before falling asleep was the wind outside and her softly saying, "Sleep tight, my dear boy. May God grant you pleasant dreams."

I slept soundly for most of the night but awoke well before daylight. Not wanting to awaken Miss Carrie I did not leave my bedroom but got out of bed, wrapped a quilt around me and sat by the window.

The sky was clear, and the moon was full casting glimmering shadows on the fresh snow and on the river. The scene seemed surreal to me, and I wondered if I would ever see such beauty again. The fear of returning to the orphanage was repressive and made me long even more for the comfortable life I could have with Miss Carrie. Of course, I told myself, she was old and might die before I was grown and was a hermit and all; but she was kind, and she loved me. To me that was all that mattered.

I must have fallen asleep in the chair by the window, because the next thing I knew I was being gently nudged by Miss Carrie.

"Wake up, sleepy head," she said. "Old Sweet Pea has fixed you the best pancakes you have ever eaten. She

also has hot fluffy biscuits and sorghum molasses. Come
get it while it's hot."

I quickly dressed and hurried downstairs and into
the kitchen. Miss Carrie and Marshal were sitting at the
table drinking coffee, and Lounicey was standing at the
stove.

"Good morning, Master Ben," she said. "I wouldn't
let Miss Carrie or Marshal have nothin' to eat till you
come down. I was afeared they would eat it all up."

All three of the adults laughed, but I did not. "I'm
scared, Miss Carrie. I'm scared I'm gonna have to go back.
I heard you tell Mr. Phillips it didn't matter what it costs
to get me to live with you. What if it costs too much? I
don't want you to be poorer than you are."

Lounicey broke out in a hearty laugh, and Miss Carrie
grinned.

"Lawdy, boy," said Lounicey. "Miss Carrie rich. She the
richest woman in town an' maybe even the whole state.
She could buy an' sell everbody in this whole town."

"Now don't go overboard, Lounicey," said Miss Carrie.
"Ben, it's true I have plenty of money. I own several oil
wells and a lot of timber land. But, dear Ben, I'd spend it
all if I had to just to see you happy. Now don't you worry
about a thing. I'm sure H. David can convince the judge to
let you live with me."

For the first time since I ran away from the orphanage
I had reason to hope.

Shortly after breakfast there was a knock on the door.

Lounicey opened the door and let Mr. Phillips in. He stomped his feet getting snow off his boots. Lounicey took his coat and shook the snow off on the porch.

Miss Carrie said, "Come in H. David. Would you like some breakfast?"

"No thank you," he said, "I've just finished eating, but I sure would like a cup of that hot coffee."

"You takes it black, don't you?" asked Lounicey.

"Black as midnight on a moonless sky," he replied.

"Well sit yourself down an' I'll pour you a cup."

"Do you have news, H. David?" asked Miss Carrie.

"I do, but don't you think we need to talk in private?"

"I have no secrets from Ben. He's a big boy. He can hear what you have to say."

"All right then," he said. "The hearing is scheduled for tomorrow. It's not going to be easy. That Pearl Greene is dead set on Ben going back to the orphanage, and she has a lot of influence on Judge Harrison. I can't get her to budge, but I'll do my best with the judge.

"You need to send Lounicey or Marshal to the Star to buy him a suit of clothes. Or better yet, I'll take him so they can fit him right. I'm afraid money is just not going to do it in this case, particularly with old Pearl raising Cain."

I was distressed and very fearful, but I kept silent.

"H. David, I mean it. I want this boy to live with me," forcefully stated Miss Carrie.

H. David looked away and scratched his head. He took out his handkerchief and blew his nose. After folding his handkerchief neatly and placing it in his pocket he looked up and said, "Then you'll have to do something you don't want to do."

By the time he finished his coffee and chatting with Miss Carrie and Lounicey it was almost nine. Mr. Phillips looked at me and said, "Come on boy, get your boots on and a heavy coat and let's us go to the Star and make you look like a movie star."

"I don't have any boots. All I have is the shoes I wore," I replied.

Miss Carrie spoke up, "Buy him some boots, some Sunday shoes and some everyday shoes. Also buy him some everyday clothes as well as a suit. And get him a heavier coat and a warm cap. Write a check on my account to pay for it. I don't want it charged."

"Miss Carrie," I said, "I don't need all that."

"Yes you do, Ben. Now don't you mind. I told you I'm going to take care of you, and I am," she said rather sternly yet soft.

So I wrapped up as best I could, and waded through the heavy snow to his car with Mr. Phillips. We went to the Star for clothes and to Magness Shoe Store for boots and shoes. Mr. Phillips wrote a check at both stores. I had never had so much stuff in all my life.

While being fitted for trousers in the Star, I was confused and then embarrassed when Mr. Lockwood asked me which side I dressed on.

"I don't know what you mean, Mr. Lockwood," I said.

He laughed and said, "Which pant leg does it hang in?"

Mr. Phillips just grinned and said, "At his age I doubt it hangs." They both laughed.

I said, "On the left," and they laughed even more.

When we got back to Miss Carrie's it was almost noon, and Amy was there.

"Amy!" I exclaimed.

"Hi, Ben. I heard on the radio that you had run away from the orphanage. Are you gonna be able to stay or do you have to go back?" she asked.

"I don't know," I said. "Miss Carrie and Mr. Phillips are gonna see if I can stay and live with Miss Carrie. We go to the courthouse tomorrow."

"Oh, I hope you can stay," she said.

"Don't you fret none, girl. Miss Carrie hardheaded enough to get her way. He gonna be able to stay," said Lounicey.

"Don't get your hopes up too much," said Miss Carrie. "We're going to do our best. You kids bundle up good and go out and play in the snow. You might never see this much snow again. I imagine it's about a foot deep. Look in the shed out back. There's an old sled in there that I had when I was a little girl. You all take it out and have fun out back, but don't go near the river and don't go anywhere that you can be seen from the street. Lounicey will call you in when lunch is ready."

As we were going out the door Lounicey said, "You oughta give Amy a hug, Ben."

"Hush up, Sweet Pea, you're embarrassing them," said Miss Carrie.

I was embarrassed and said nothing, but I really did want to give her a hug.

Amy was appropriately dressed for playing in the snow. I went to my bedroom, took all my new clothes and dressed warmly in my boots, heavy coat and wool cap we had just purchased.

As we opened the kitchen door Miss Carrie said, "You children be careful and remember to keep out of sight from the street."

"Yes ma'am," we both said as we left the warmth of the house.

It took awhile to find the sled among all the junk packed for years in the shed. When we finally found it we saw that, though rusty and dirty, it was usable.

Next to the path I had always used to come to the house was another path that sloped downward toward the river. About ten yards from the bluff bank of the river the path turned sharply to the right, continued to slope downward for a short distance and then had a gradual slope upwards for another fifteen or twenty yards.

"Let's slide down that path," said Amy.

"Okay, but if we don't make that turn we'll end up in the river. With all these heavy clothes on we'll drown for sure," I said, wanting to take no chance of injury.

"Don't be chicken," laughed Amy. "If we don't make the turn all we have to do is fall off the sled into the snow. Come on."

I was hesitant but didn't want to be afraid. She got on the front of the sled; and I sat behind with her sitting between my legs. I pushed off and Amy guided the sled. Sure enough we were unable to negotiate the turn, and

Amy froze in place. I grabbed her around the chest and pulled her off the sled with me. We rolled and tumbled and slid, finally coming to rest less than a yard from the bluff bank. The sled crashed into the river and was soon out of sight.

"Dadgummit Amy, we near 'bout got killed," I said.

She just laughed.

I worried about losing Miss Carrie's sled, but I knew she wouldn't mind. We began making a snowman, but before we could finish Lounicey called us in for lunch. Amy said she had to go home or her mother would worry about her.

"Okay," I said, "but can you come back after you eat?"

"I'll try, but if I can't I'll see you in court tomorrow unless they have school. If they have school I'll come after school."

"I just hope I'm here," I said. "I'm scared of what the judge will do."

I watched her walk down the path until she was out of sight and wondered if this would be the last time I would see her. Then I turned and went in for lunch.

After lunch I sat by the fire with Miss Carrie. We said nothing but just watched the flames. Soon I dozed off, and when I awoke she was still sitting there looking at me with a strange look in her eyes.

"What's the matter, Miss Carrie?" I asked.

"Nothing, child. I was just admiring how handsome you are. I hope I live long enough to see you grown. I was

wondering what you'll be. I hope you come back here to
Fabre's Bluff and take care of all my affairs."

"I will, Miss Carrie. I love it here ever since I met you."

"What a nice thing to say," she said. "Ben, I know you
are worried about tomorrow, but don't be. I promise I will
do whatever it takes to keep you with me. I want you to be
my little boy, the child I never had. I'm old but not too old."

Finally I felt confident and at peace. I had lost my
mother when I was born and my father in the war. My
grandmother died of a broken heart, and I was alone. But
I knew that as long as Miss Carrie lived I would not be
alone. I didn't feel like an orphan anymore.

By mid-afternoon the sun had come out, and the snow
began to melt. Amy did not return, and that caused some
concern for me.

I needed something to take my mind off the next
day's court appearance so I went through Miss Carrie's
bookshelf looking for something to read. I picked the old
poetry book and started reading Evangeline, but well into
it I found it too sad, so I put it back and went outside.

It was warmer than the morning, and the sun felt good
on my face. Wandering down the path to the river I saw
the sled washed up on a sandbar. I walked through the
snow along the edge of the bluff taking care not to stumble
and fall in the river. After about ten yards I reached the
snow-covered sandbar and pulled the sled out of the water.
It was not damaged.

The trip back up the bank was difficult, particularly

the path up the bluff; but I made it without falling. I placed the sled back on the shelf and went inside.

"Where have you been, child?" asked Miss Carrie.

"I went to the edge of the bluff and saw the sled had washed up, so I went down to the river and got it. I put it back in the shed," I replied.

"Ben, that was too dangerous in this snow. Don't you do that again. I mean it," said Miss Carrie.

It felt nice to have someone care enough about me to fuss at me.

After dinner that evening Miss Carrie invited me into the living room and drew up two chairs and a small table by the fire. "Come and sit, Ben. I'm going to teach you how to play gin."

I took a seat across the table and said, "I know how to play gin. My dad taught me. I'll bet I can beat you, Miss Carrie," I said.

She laughed and shook her finger at me and said, "I'll bet you can't, young man. Lounicey and I play all the time, and I always win."

I laughed and said, "I'll bet old Sweet Pea just lets you win."

"All right, smarty pants, we'll see," and she began shuffling the cards.

We played each game to a hundred, and she won three out of four games. After the fifth game she said, "Dear boy, it's time for bed. Sleep tight and don't let the bed bugs bite."

She pulled me to her and gave me a really tight hug. When she released me she said, "Don't you worry, child, it's going to be all right."

I went to my room, undressed and got in bed. The curtains were open, and the moon was full, casting a bright light into the room. There was a moderate breeze outside causing a quivering of shadows of the bare limbs outside cast on the ceiling by the moonlight. I lay on my back fascinated by the moving shadows, warm under the heavy quilts, and hoped above hope that this could be my home forever.

Soon I fell into a sound sleep full of pleasant dreams. I was awakened at dawn by the sound of a crowing rooster. Today was to be the most important day of my life.

Jumping out of bed I put on socks and slipped my feet in my boots without tying the laces. I went in the water closet, emptied my bladder, washed my face, and combed my hair. When I came downstairs Lounicey was at the stove cooking and Miss Carrie was sitting at the table drinking coffee.

"Hurry and dress, Ben," Miss Carrie said. "Mr. Phillips will be here shortly. Put on your new clothes but not your necktie. Bring it down with you, and I'll tie it for you after you eat."

I rushed upstairs, dressed as instructed and came back down to the kitchen. Mr. Phillips was sitting at the table drinking coffee beside Miss Carrie.

"Sit yourself, boy," said Lounicey. "I'm fixin' you some

ham an' eggs and biscuits an' honey. Here's a glass of
orange juice I just squeezed."

"I'm not too hungry, Lounicey. Just give me a biscuit
and honey, "I said.

"Nonsense, boy, you gotta eat. You lookin' at a long
day ahead of you. I'm not gonna let you go out on a empty
stomach."

So I sat and ate what she put in front of me, and it was
good.

When I was through eating Miss Carrie tied my
necktie on me and gave me a hug. She said nothing but
just looked at me lovingly.

Mr. Phillips said, "Lounicey, you get in your Model A
and be at the courthouse no later than nine. When they
open the courtroom door you come in and take a seat in
the back where you can see me and where you can get out
quick if I signal you."

Lounicey said, "Yessir, Lawyer Phillips, I know what to
do."

I wondered if they were gonna run away with me if it
didn't look good, but I didn't ask.

"Okay, big boy, let's us get going and show 'em how the
cow ate the cabbage," said Mr. Phillips as he put on his
coat and hat.

Miss Carrie straightened my hair down and said,
"It's gonna be okay. Don't you be afraid. You sit up there
and look that judge straight in the eye and answer his
questions truthfully."

I hugged her and went out the door with Mr. Phillips.
We got in his Ford and headed for the biggest day of my
life.

Typical of Arkansas weather the day was clear and much warmer than the freezing temperature of forty-eight hours earlier. The sky was clear, and the sun was bright. What had been a beautiful snowscape was now just dirty melting slush.

For the first time in my twelve years I was dressed in a coat and tie. I felt as though I would soon be perspiring in the warm car. On top of that, my new dress shoes were hurting my feet. All of that made my mood turn somber instead of the excited feeling I had earlier experienced.

On the way, Mr. Phillips gave me instructions. "Now Ben," he started. "There is no need to be nervous. Just answer the judge's questions honestly and briefly. Do not elaborate."

"What does elaborate mean?" I asked.

"It means to expound on a subject."

"What does expound mean?"

"Well, it means to explain something or answer a question in too much detail. For example, if someone asked you what color the sky was you would say blue. But if you elaborated or expounded you would say mostly it's blue but sometimes it is gray when there is fog or clouds, and at night it's black unless there is a bright moon, and then it's light black, but if there is no moon you can see lots of stars, so it's a lot of different colors," he explained.

"Oh," I said, but I wondered why he didn't just tell me to not talk too much.

"Mr. Phillips, will there be a bunch of people there?" I asked.

"I don't know," he replied. "Most times there is no one in the audience, but you have become sort of a celebrity, so there may be a fairly large crowd."

When we arrived at the courthouse and parked the car, I noticed a small group of people standing around the main entrance. As we walked past them some acknowledged us, and some just stared. I became very nervous, more so when we got inside and saw many people gathered in the hallway.

When we got to the courtroom a man in a uniform opened the door for us. The room was empty. Mr. Phillips led me through a small gate and had me sit at a large table. He sat beside me, smiled and patted me on the knee. "It'll be okay," he said.

When I heard the doors open and people coming in I turned and looked. I was disturbed when I saw Mr. Baker, Miss Claudia, and the janitor from the orphanage enter and take seats.

"What are they doing here?" I asked Mr. Phillips.

"The judge will just ask them some questions, and then they'll leave," he replied. "Don't worry, and no matter what they say keep your mouth shut!"

After everyone was settled in their seats the man in uniform told us all to stand and said, "This court is now in session, the Honorable Marcus Harrison presiding."

Then a side door opened, and a big fat man in a black robe came in and sat behind the large desk at the front of the room. He looked mean. Now I was really scared.

The judge sat at his desk for several minutes adjusting papers. Finally he looked up, banged a little wooden hammer on his desk and said, "Ladies and gentleman, I must admit I am surprised to see so many people in the audience. I want to inform you that this is not a trial. It is merely a hearing for me to decide what to do about this orphaned boy, Benjamin Williams.

"The decision will be mine and mine alone. I will tolerate no outbursts from the audience. Although it is not a trial I still have the authority to hold anyone in contempt of court, and be assured I will. I will call all witnesses and will ask all the questions. Benjamin is in court and is represented by H. David Phillips.

"There are some officials of the orphanage in Little Rock in attendance. Since they have driven all this way in this foul weather I will hear them early and let them be on their way.

"But first I will hear from Miss Pearl Greene."

Miss Greene came to the bench and took a seat in the witness chair. The man in the deputy uniform approached her with a Bible in his hand and said, "Raise your right hand and place your left hand on the Bible."

She did, and he said, "Do you solemnly swear to tell the truth, the whole truth, and nothing but the truth?"

"I do," she said.

"State your name and occupation," he said.

"I'm Pearl Greene, and I'm the social worker for the State of Arkansas Child Welfare Department assigned to this county."

"Miss Greene," said the judge, "state what you know about this case."

"Well, Your Honor, it came to my attention this boy, Ben Williams, was an orphan. He had no mother and his father was killed in the war. He was living with his grandmother, Narcissa Guillaume. Mrs. Guillaume was in poor health, and Ben had to fend for himself. The state was preparing to take him out of that house and place him in a foster home when word came from the sheriff that his grandmother had died.

"Since there was no time to find foster parents, I went and got him and took him to the orphanage. I didn't know anything else to do. I couldn't let a twelve year old boy live alone."

"How did Ben feel about that?" asked the judge.

"Well, he just didn't want to go. He claimed he had someone he could live with, but he wouldn't tell me who."

The judge looked at Mr. Phillips and asked, "Do you want to question Miss Greene, Mr. Phillips?"

"Just one question, Your Honor. Miss Greene, I understand that you took this boy to the orphanage within an hour or two after his grandmother died. Is that true?"

"It is," she replied.

"And you didn't even let him stay here long enough to attend her funeral. Is that true?"

"Well, yes sir, but I didn't have anything else to do with him," she said.

"I would imagine you could have thought of something. I have no more questions of this woman," Mr. Phillips said sort of sarcastically.

"You may step down," said the judge.

Miss Greene stepped down and walked past us, giving us a dirty look as she went by.

Judge Harrison looked at me and had a strange look
on his face. It was almost a smile but not quite, more
like a look of someone feeling sorry for another person.
It confused me, and I looked at Mr. Phillips, but he just
looked toward the judge. Frequently he looked toward the
back of the room. After he looked for about the fifth time
he smiled. I looked toward the direction of his gaze and
saw Lounicey and Marshal standing against the back wall.

Judge Harrison said, "Mr. James Baker, I believe you
have something to say. Please come forward."

Mr. Baker approached the bench, sat in the witness
chair and was sworn in.

"The floor is yours, sir, say your piece," said the judge.

"Your Honor, my name is James Baker, and I'm the
superintendent of the state orphanage in Little Rock. We
had in residence there Ben Williams, a twelve year old
orphan from this city. He was there for just over three
months.

"During that time we had no trouble with him at all.
He seemed well adjusted. He did have a fight at school but
had no other problems there.

"I was surprised when he ran away. I was informed by
Miss Claudia Bailey, the evening supervisor, of his leaving
us. We immediately notified the authorities, but they
were unsuccessful in finding Ben. Miss Bailey can tell you
the circumstances of his escape."

"I have no questions for you, Mr. Baker. What about
you, Mr. Phillips?"

"No questions, Your Honor, but I do find it interesting
that Mr. Baker described Ben's leaving as his escape."

There was a stir from the audience and muffled
laughter.

"There will be none of that," sternly admonished the

judge. "Miss Bailey, come forward please."

She took her seat in the witness chair, was sworn in and said, "It's Mrs. Bailey, judge. I am married, you know. The children call me Miss Claudia. That's where the confusion comes from."

"I'll be sure to address you correctly, Mrs. Bailey (and he emphasized the Mrs.), but you will address me as Your Honor and not judge. Do you understand?"

Her face became flushed, and she gritted her teeth and said, "Yes sir."

"Well, say what you have to say," said the judge.

"From day one, this boy let me know he didn't want to be there and certainly did not appreciate what we did for him," she said.

"Now wait a minute, Mrs. Bailey. Did he cause you any trouble? Was he a problem? Did he require discipline, and if so, what?" asked Judge Harrison.

"No," she said.

"No, what?" asked the judge.

"No sir," said Miss Claudia.

There were a few giggles that stopped when the judge sternly looked up.

"That's not what I mean, Mrs. Bailey. I asked if he caused trouble or required discipline. I wanted you to answer each of those points. No – did he cause trouble, and No- did he require discipline."

"No to both," she said, through clenched teeth.

"Do you have anything to add?" asked the judge.

"No," she said, "but I would like for Chester Johnson, our janitor, to tell you what that boy did to escape, I mean run away," she said.

"All right, unless Mr. Phillips wants to question you, you may be excused." He looked at Mr. Phillips who shook his head no. "You may step down," said the judge.

She walked off in a huff and went straight to the door and out of the courtroom.

"Mr. Johnson, come forward, be seated and take the oath," said Judge Harrison.

Chester was given the oath. His voice was unsteady, and his right hand shook when he raised it. I felt sorry for him. He was a nice man, and all the boys liked him. I hated to see him so intimidated.

"Mr. Johnson, please don't be nervous or frightened. I do not mean to intimidate you. We are all friends here. Just relax. Now tell us what happened in your own words. Take your time," said the judge in softer tones than he had used all morning.

"Well sir," Chester started, "this little boy is a good boy. He's always been very polite. He's the only one there, children and adults alike, that says sir to me. I don't feel bad about what he done."

"That's well and good, Mr. Johnson," said the judge, "but just tell us what happened."

"Yes sir. Well I was comin' down the hall that Friday night when Ben come up to me and said somebody throwed up at the far end of the hall. I said I'd clean it up. I told him to go to his room, but he said he had to go to the john. He went into the john, and I went next door and got a bucket, a mop, and filled the bucket with water.

"I guess I left the storeroom door open, and as I was goin' down the hall he must of slipped in. Well, I got to the far end of the hall and sure 'nuff there was a big wad of puke on the floor. I cleaned it up and mopped the spot where it were and went back to the john and flushed the puke down the commode. Then I put my mop and bucket back in the storeroom and turned out the light and locked the door when I went out.

"He must of snuck in the storeroom and hid while I was cleaning up the puke, because the next morning we found the winder open. He must of throwed his bag out the winder and climbed down the tree to get out. I'll bet he planned the whole thing and even puked on the floor so he could get in the storeroom. That's where the only winder without a screen on it was."

"Sounds like a pretty smart plan to me," said the judge. There was laughter, but this time the judge said nothing.

"Do you have any questions, H. David?" asked the judge.

"No, Your Honor," replied Mr. Phillips.

"All right, Mr. Johnson, you may step down. All you Little Rock people can leave now. You're excused."

"But, Your Honor, we need to stay to take Ben back," said Mr. Baker.

"Mr. Baker, I said you are excused. If I send Ben back, Mr. Phillips will bring him. Goodbye, sir," said Judge Harrison.

The orphanage people left, but the only one who was ready to go was Chester Johnson.

"Mr. Phillips, do you have any other witness you want

me to question before I talk with your young client?" asked the judge.

"No, Your Honor, I don't," replied H. David.

"All right, Master Ben, it's your turn. Come on up and have a seat," said Judge Harrison.

As I started to rise from my chair, Mr. Phillips whispered, "It'll be okay, Ben, just tell the truth and keep your answers short."

I said nothing but got up, walked toward the bench and sat in the witness chair. The uniformed man approached and held out a Bible. "Place your left hand on the Bible and raise your right hand," he said. "Do you solemnly swear to tell the truth, the whole truth, and nothing but the truth?"

"Yes sir," I replied.

"Your name is Benjamin Williams, isn't it son?" asked the judge.

"How old are you?"

"I'm twelve. I'll be thirteen on my birthday," I replied.

"And when is your birthday?"

"It's June the twenty-second, Your Honorable," I replied. That brought about laughter from even the judge. I was embarrassed.

"It's Your Honor, son," said the judge with a grin. "But I'll tell you what. All my friends call me Marc, and I want to be your friend. Why don't you just call me Judge Marc? Is that okay with you?"

"Yes sir," I replied. I was beginning to relax and actually like the judge.

"Now, before we start, do you see that door over there?" and he pointed past me to a door near the wall behind where juries would sit.

"Yes sir," I replied.

"Through that door is my private office. Would you rather just you and I go in that office where we can talk in private?"

"No sir, this is just fine in here."

"All right, let's get started. For the record, you are Benjamin Williams, age twelve. That's what you told me. Right?"

"Yes sir, but everybody calls me Ben."

"Okay, Ben it is. Now, Ben, you heard Mr. Johnson testify. Is what he said true?"

"Yes sir," I replied.

"Who vomited?" asked the judge.

"I did."

"Were you sick?"

"No sir."

"Well why did you vomit? Tell me the whole story."

"Yes sir. Well, I worked out a plan. Before supper I packed my suitcase, and while everybody else went down to eat I hid it in the bathroom along with my coat. Then I went downstairs and ate all my supper. Randy and Sammy didn't eat all theirs---"

"Wait a minute, Ben," said Judge Marc, "who are Randy and Sammy?"

"They were my roommates."

"Oh, go on."

"They left some food on their plates, so I ate it and some the other boys left on their plates too. I was so full I was about to bust."

There was some muffled laughter that stopped when the judge held up his hand and gave the audience a dirty look.

"I was going to ask why you ate so much, but I think I'm about to get the picture. Go on."

"We went back to our room, and Randy and Sammy promised not to tell on me, but they said I was crazy. But I didn't care, I just wanted out of there and back here."

"Why did you choose a Friday night?" interrupted the judge.

"Because Saturday was no school, and everybody could sleep late."

"That was using your head," said Judge Marc. "Go on."

"I knew Mr. Johnson would come down the hall about eight. So when I heard him coming up the stairs I ran my finger down my throat and threw up on the floor. I showed it to Mr. Johnson, and he told me to go to my room, but I told him I had to go to the bathroom. He said okay, so I went there but kept the door cracked where I could see him.

"When he came out of the storeroom with his stuff, I got my stuff and went into the storeroom and hid under a big table. In a little bit he came back and put his stuff up. After he turned out the light and locked the door behind him I waited a little bit 'til I knew he'd be gone, and I opened the window and dropped my bag in some bushes down below. Then I jumped into a tree and climbed down and picked up my bag and took off running."

"That sounds like a pretty smart plan. Now how did you get to Fabre's Bluff?"

"I figured if I went south on the road I'd probably get caught, so I crossed the river to North Little Rock and went to the train yard and climbed in a boxcar on a train that started moving to the south.

"A man named Little Sam jumped in after I did and helped me cover up with straw to stay warm. Boy it was cold! When we got to Gurdon the train slowed down and Little Sam said I'd better jump while I could, so I did.

"I walked through town and got a ride with a man in a wagon to Chidester. I took off walking down the road, and a man on a horse came along and gave me a ride to Maul. I walked the rest of the way here."

"That was some odyssey, young man. When you got here where did you go?"

"To a lady's house," I said.

"What lady? What's her name?" he asked.

"I can't tell you that, Judge Marc," I said.

"Why not?"

"I just can't, that's all."

"If I order you to tell me, you're saying you won't. Is that right?"

"Yes sir, that's right," I replied.

"At least tell me why you won't tell me."

"Because the lady is bashful and doesn't like to be around people," I said.

"Young man, I cannot just turn you loose in this town not knowing where or with whom you will be living. H. David, I'm going to call a recess for thirty minutes. During that time you talk to your client and explain things to him. The court will recess for thirty minutes," the judge said, and he hit his desk with a wooden hammer, got up and walked through the door to his office.

As I was walking toward Mr. Phillips I saw him nod at Lounicey, and she left the courtroom.

As I approached Mr. Phillips rose from his chair, straightened his tie, and said, "Come on, Ben, let's go in the jury room."

I followed him into a large room in the center of which was a long table with twelve leather chairs around it. There were five chairs along the inside wall and a long credenza between the two windows of the outside wall.

"Have a seat and relax, boy. Lean back, take your shoes off, and put your feet up on the table."

I did as he suggested. It felt good to get the new shoes off and my feet up. I had mixed feelings. I was tired yet excited but also afraid.

"What's gonna happen to me, Mr. Phillips?" I asked. "I'm getting scared."

"Well, Ben, it's like this. Judge Harrison isn't going to turn you, a twelve year old boy, loose to live on your own. You've got to have an adult to take you in. I would do it, but with five kids at home my wife would have a fit if I brought another one in. It's just a good thing I was 4-F because of my flat feet and asthma or she would have been in a pickle.

"But don't you fret; I've still got another card up my sleeve."

There was a knock on the door and then it opened. The man in the uniform said, "It's time, Lawyer Phillips. You all come on back in the courtroom."

As we walked toward our seats I noticed Lounicey and Marshal standing in the back of the room leaning against the wall. Lounicey nodded at Mr. Phillips, and he smiled.

Judge Harrison entered, and everyone stood up until

he sat down.

He banged his hammer and said, "Mr. Phillips, has your client decided to be more forthcoming with the court?"

"No, Your Honor, he has not, but I have a final witness who can clear it all up." He waved at Lounicey, and she opened the main door and went into the hall.

In a moment Lounicey opened the door and Miss Carrie walked in. I was shocked! I had never seen her look so fine. Her white hair was pulled back in a bun. She was wearing a light blue business-type suit, the skirt of which came down well below her knees. She had on a cream-colored blouse with a fluffy scarf at the neck. Her mid-heel shoes matched her suit, and she was wearing hose.

She came to our table, smiled at me, and stood beside Mr. Phillips who said, "Your Honor, I believe this lady can shed all the light you need on this subject."

"Madam," the judge said, "please come take a seat in the witness chair and be sworn in."

The court officer gave Miss Carrie the usual oath.

The judge said, "Please state your name, age, and address for the court."

"My name is Carlotta Stephens, but those who know me call me Carrie. I am seventy-nine years old but healthy as a horse. I live at One Bluff Road in the house that appears from the outside to be dilapidated. I think I am commonly known as the old witch lady who lives in the haunted house."

There were audible gasps from the audience, and even Judge Harrison seemed to be taken aback.

"Mrs. Stephens," the judge began.

Miss Carrie interrupted, "It's Miss, Your Honor. I've never been married."

"Miss Stephens," the judge resumed, "please tell the court why you are here. Take your time. You'll not be interrupted. When you are finished, I may have questions for you."

"Thank you, Your Honor." She paused for almost a minute as though she was trying to think of what to say. The judge said nothing.

Finally she said, "When I was eighteen a great tragedy befell me, the details of which are of no concern to this court. Suffice it to say I was greatly hurt and bereaved by it, so much so that I had no desire to live. But I could not die because I had much to live for. The hurt was so bad that I gradually decided to divorce the world, so to speak. I stopped going out in public and wanted the public to leave me alone.

"In my mid-twenties my father died, and I was alone, except for my friends and helpers, Lounicey and Marshal Porter, who have stood by me all these years.

"I let my property and house deteriorate to discourage company, and it worked. Oh, I had, and still have, many nice things inside to comfort me. The site of the house, I have been told, is on the spot where Jacque Fabre had his trading post. I am, by the way, a direct descendant of Fabre.

"For the past sixty-one years I have been a recluse. The only time I leave my property has always been late at night when Lounicey rides me around town in her Model A. I keep up with what goes on through the radio, the newspaper, and word of mouth from the Porters, Mr. Phillips, and Mr. Rankin who is my tax man in Little Rock."

Everyone, including the judge, was listening intently.

"On Halloween night 1941, this young man, Ben

Williams, came into my life. From that day on he has been
in my home almost daily. He has brought great joy to me;
and, if I may say so, I to him. He has a key to my house
and knows he is welcome at any time.

"He has even brought his girlfriend to see me." She
smiled and winked at me which made me blush.

"So you see, this young man has given me something to
live for. You might say he has given me my life back. If you
will please let him live with me, I promise I will attend the
PTA, have him in the Methodist Church every Sunday,
and attend every activity he is in. When the time comes I
will send him to college.

"Also, I will repair the outside of my house and keep up
the property as well as I have the inside. Please let him
live with me. I love him, and he loves me."

The entire room was quiet. Finally the judge spoke,
"Miss Stephens, can you afford to raise this child?"

"Your Honor, I am quite wealthy. I own over ten
thousand acres of timberland from which about seven
hundred and fifty acres a year are cut. Some timber goes
to sawmills, and some is cut into billets and sold to the
paper mill. I also have fifteen producing oil wells. I can
have Mr. Rankin produce proof of all I have stated."

The judge looked shocked and looked at Mr. Phillips,
who just nodded.

Judge Harrison said, "So when Ben ran away from the
orphanage he came to you."

"Yes sir, he did. In fact, he came here from my house
with Mr. Phillips this morning."

"My God," the judge exclaimed, "he came by boxcar,
wagon, and horseback through cold and wet snow to be
with you. What an odyssey for such a brave young man.
Ben, do you want to live with Miss Stephens?"

"Yes sir," I shouted.

"So be it then. It is the order of this court that you
are to be in her charge until you reach your majority." He
banged his gavel and declared, "This court is dismissed.
Mr. Phillips, draw up the papers, and I'll sign them."

Miss Carrie and I came together at once in a big hug.
Both of us were crying.

We left the courtroom arm in arm and followed Mr.
Phillips to his car. I sat in the front seat between Miss
Carrie and him. All three of us were laughing as we drove
down the street.

Miss Carrie looked at me, winked and said, "H. David,
now that I am no longer an old hermit witch I need to
learn to drive a car. Will you teach me?"

"I'd be glad to," he replied.

"All right then," she said, "you can teach me in your
car, and as soon as the war is over and they start making
them again, I'm going to buy a Buick from Mr. Hornaday.
I don't care if it is so long you have to back it up to get it to
turn a corner!"

"Now don't go that far, Carrie. You'd be better off
buying a smaller car like a Chevrolet or a Ford," Mr.
Phillips said with a laugh.

"Well, what about you, big boy," said Miss Carrie,
"what would you like?"

"Whatever you want, Miss Carrie, is okay with me. I've
got what I want. I'm not an orphan anymore."

She pulled me to her and hugged me tightly as her

eyes welled up with tears.

When we reached the house it was late afternoon. Miss Carrie invited Mr. Phillips to have dinner with us, and he accepted.

Miss Carrie said, "H. David, I know you have other matters that need your attention. Go ahead with them but be back here at six for supper."

"I'll be here with bells on," he said with a grin.

We watched him drive away and then walked down the cobblestone sidewalk to the front porch. As we walked across the porch to the front door she said, "Dear Ben, the last time you entered the house through this door you were covered with eggs."

We both laughed, and she put her arms around me and had the most tender look in her eyes. She said, "For the rest of your life you will be able to come in the front door for all to see. And it won't look like this much longer. I have talked to Harrison Todd about tearing away all the bad wood and bricks and completely refinishing the outside to be as nice looking as the inside. Of course he will have to wait until the war is over to get the building supplies."

"You don't have to do that for me, Miss Carrie," I protested.

"Oh, but I do, dear Ben, but also for me. I've been a hermit far too long. You've given me my life back, and I love you for it. Now run on off and tell Amy your good news, but first look on the side porch. "

I did as she said, and there stood a perfectly good second-hand bicycle.

"Where did you find that, Miss Carrie? Is it for me? My old bike is worn out."

"Of course it is, child. You don't think I'm going to ride it, do you? Marshal found it over in his neighborhood. Now hop on it and go find Amy."

The sun was low in the west but still bright. Much of the snow had melted, and the slush left on the street made riding the bicycle difficult. After slipping and sliding a bit I got off the bike and pushed it along.

When I got to Amy's and knocked there was no answer for the longest. As I turned to leave, the door opened and there stood Mrs. McDonald with tears in her eyes.

She wiped her tears away with her apron and said, "Come on in, Ben. Amy is in the living room."

I found Amy sitting on the couch. She was sobbing. I looked at Mrs. McDonald. She said, "We just got a telegram telling us that Amy's daddy is missing."

"Missing?" I asked.

"Missing in action. He hasn't been seen since the battle in Bastogne."

I sat beside Amy and took her hand in mine. "I know how you feel, Amy, because I got a telegram, or rather Granny did, that told us about Daddy getting killed. But this just said he was missing. Maybe he's just a prisoner or something. It didn't say he was dead."

"I know he's dead," she sobbed. "I just know it."

"No you don't. You've still got hope. Don't give up.
I bet he's in a prison camp and doing fine. Just keep
thinking that."

"I'll try, Ben. Oh, what about court? Are they going to
let you live with Miss Carrie?" she asked, wiping her face.

"Yes they are! You wouldn't believe it, Amy. Miss
Carrie walked into that courtroom all dressed up and told
the judge all about her house and how rich she was and
how she wanted me, and he let her have me. I belong to
her now. I'm not an orphan anymore."

Both Amy and her mother hugged me although they
were still crying. It almost made me cry.

"Keep hoping, Mrs. McDonald, and you too, Amy. If he
had got killed they would have known it and would have
told you," I said as I got up to leave. "I've got to go home
now. Supper is about ready, but I'll be back tomorrow
after school. I've got to get back in school."

"Did you hear what you said, Ben?" asked Mrs.
McDonald.

"What do you mean, ma'am?" I asked.

"You said you had to go home," she replied. "You've got
a home now."

I did have a home; I realized it now. I hopped on my
bike and hurried home, my home with Miss Carrie.

"Why were you gone so long, Ben? We thought you had
run away from home," she said, looking at Mr. Phillips and
winking.

"Oh, Miss Carrie, Amy and her mother just found out

that Mr. McDonald was missing. They were afraid he was dead."

"That's terrible," she said, "but maybe he is just in a prison camp and is okay."

"That's what I said to them. They said they'd try to think that way."

Miss Carrie said, "Good boy. H. David, why don't you get in your car and go bring them here for supper. You go with him, Ben. They don't need to be alone."

Mr. Phillips agreed and said, "Come on, Ben."

On the way to Amy's, Mr. Phillips said, "Ben, you are a very lucky boy to have Miss Carrie; but she's even luckier than you."

"Why?" I asked.

"Because she's got you, someone she can love and care for, someone who brought her out of her shell, something to live for."

I never thought of that. All I knew was I loved Miss Carrie and she loved me.

When we arrived at Amy's house, Mr. Phillips knocked on the door.

Mrs. McDonald opened the door, and Mr. Phillips said, "Ma'am, Ben told us your news. Miss Stephens doesn't want you to be alone. She sent Ben and me to fetch you to supper with us."

"Oh, we couldn't, Mr. Phillips, we wouldn't be fit company. You all need to celebrate your good fortune from today."

"Nonsense, Mrs. McDonald. She will have her feelings hurt if you don't come," he said.

"Yes ma'am," I said. "Please come."

"Let's go Mom," said Amy. "I don't want us to be alone."

"All right then," said Mrs. McDonald. "Let us get our coats."

We waited just inside the door. In a very short time Amy and her mother appeared wearing their coats. Amy also was wearing a knit cap. Mrs. McDonald took Amy by the right hand, and Amy took my hand with her other.

On the way to Miss Carrie's, Mr. Phillips looked at Amy's mother in the rearview mirror. "Mrs. McDonald," he started.

She interrupted and said, "Please call me Mary."

He replied, "Only if you will call me H. David. But ma'am, I truly believe your husband is alive. I've read about the battle at Bastogne. Our troops were surrounded and thus well accounted for. Had he been killed surely he would have been accounted for. His body would have been found. The fact that he wasn't found leads me to believe he was captured. It's been about two months since that battle ended. Maybe the Red Cross can help locate him. If you would like, I will contact the Red Cross tomorrow."

"Oh, please do, Mr. Phillips. Thank you so much," she said.

"H. David," he reminded.

"Yes- H. David, "she replied.

Amy sat close to her mother, softly crying. I wished I was in the back seat beside her.

Mr. Phillips parked by the front gate, and we walked to the porch and up the steps to the door. Each step creaked loudly, and once I thought a step was about to break.

The door opened before we could knock, and Miss Carrie invited us in. "I'm Carrie, and I believe your name is Mary. Of course I know young Amy," she said.

As she was taking their coats Miss Carrie said, "Mary and Amy, welcome to our home, Ben's and mine. I am so sorry it is under such distressing circumstances, but I truly believe your loved one is safe and a prisoner."

"Thank you, Miss Stephens," said Mary.

"Now Mary, I know I'm old enough to be your mother, maybe even your grandmother, but I do want you to not be so formal. Please call me Carrie. And you, Master Ben, you can drop the Miss, but we'll talk about that later."

She pulled me to her, smiled and said, "This handsome young man first came through that door on Halloween night, nineteen forty-one, all covered with eggs. I fell in love with him at once."

She winked at me. I blushed.

H. David, with his coat still on and his hat in his hand, said, "If you will excuse me, I'll be on my way."

"Nonsense," said Miss Carrie, "you will stay for supper. Go get your wife and bring her too."

"She's in El Dorado spending a few days with her sister," he replied.

"Well, just what were you going to do for supper, H. David?" she asked with a small smile on her face.

"I was going to hope you would invite me to stay," he replied.

Miss Carrie and I couldn't help laughing. Even Mrs. McDonald smiled. Amy just stood with tears in her eyes.

Miss Carrie took Amy in her arms and hugged her tightly. "Please don't fear for your daddy, dear girl. He will be all right, I just know it."

We went into the living room and sat by the fire. Mrs. McDonald scanned the room, her eyes wide. "What a lovely room," she said.

"Why, thank you, Mary," said Miss Carrie. "It's a far

sight nicer than the outside, wouldn't you say? But now
that I have my boy here, I'm going to fix up the outside
just as soon as the war is over. I left it looking dilapidated
to keep people away, and I was successful. But this young
man changed all that. He brought happiness to me and
brought me out of hibernation."

I thought I was going to cry I was so happy, although I
hurt for Amy.

"Come to supper y'all," yelled Lounicey.

"Come in and meet the rest of my family, Mary," said
Miss Carrie.

We entered the dining room, and Miss Carrie said, "Sit
anywhere you like."

The table was amply set with food. Lounicey and
Marshal came in carrying a platter full of pieces of fried
chicken, and each took a seat at the table. I detected a
surprised look on Mrs. McDonald's face, but she said
nothing.

"Mary, this is Lounicey and her husband, Marshal.
They take care of me and of Ben. They are family."

"Hello," said Mrs. McDonald.

"How do, ma'am," said Sweet Pea and Marshal in
unison.

After the meal was finished, pleasantries were
exchanged and Mrs. McDonald thanked Miss Carrie for
the hospitality and the meal and declared it was time for
Amy and her to leave.

Miss Carrie got their coats and hats and bid them

goodbye with a hug, even H. David got a hug.

We went back into the dining room and helped Lounicey clear the table.

Miss Carrie said, "Sweet Pea, after you wash the dishes just stack them on the counter. Ben and I will put them away. Go on home with Marshal and sleep late in the morning and just come in whenever you like."

She and I went into the living room. "Put another log on the fire, Sweety," she said. "Let's sit awhile."

I had never been called "Sweety" before by anyone. I liked it. It made me feel like I really belonged to her.

She patted on the sofa beside her indicating where she wanted me to sit. I sat there; and she took my hand in both of hers, looked me in the eye and said, "Ben, you are officially my little boy now. I didn't say 'my son' because I was not able to adopt you, my being single and all. But I think of you more as a grandson since I am so old, and you are so young. It just doesn't seem right, considering our new relationship, for you to keep calling me 'Miss Carrie'. What would you like to call me?"

"I don't know, Miss Carrie," I replied.

"There you go," she laughed. "Well, you can't call me 'Granny' because that's what you called your grandmother. Why don't you call me 'Nannie' or even 'Auntie'?"

I loved her, but she wasn't my grandmother. I didn't feel comfortable calling her anything like I called my grandmother. "How about 'Auntie'?" I asked.

I thought I saw a tiny indication of disappointment in her eyes. She said, "That will be all right."

"I know," I said. "Lonnie called his grandmother, the one who died, 'Mimi'. Can I call you that?"

She seemed genuinely pleased and said, "'Mimi' will be fine. From now on, dear Ben, I'm your Mimi."

I was too excited to fall asleep quickly. My room was cold so I pulled the cover up under my chin. The snow had mostly melted, the sky was clear, and the moon was full. I lay in bed and watched the moon shadows dance across the ceiling. I had a home. I had my own room and new clothes. I had Mimi who loved me. I had lost my mother at birth, my father to the war, and my grandmother to grief; but I had Miss Carrie who was now Mimi. I was going to be okay.

The next morning I was to enroll in school so I was up and dressed early. As we were eating breakfast there was a knock on the front door. Mimi excused herself and went to the door.

I heard her say, "Yes, I am Carrie Stephens, and yes, Benjamin Williams lives here. Why does that concern you?"

I left the table and went to the door. There stood Pearl Greene. She looked my way and nodded.

"This boy is an orphan, and I represent the Child Welfare department of the state," Miss Greene said. "I have come here to inspect these premises to see if it is a fit place for this boy to live."

"But the judge ruled that he could live with me and be in my care until he is grown. You have no say in that," said Miss Carrie.

"Oh, but I do," replied Miss Greene. "This boy is an orphan, and the state has a say in the welfare of orphans. Do not try to obstruct me, ma'am."

"I'm not an orphan anymore," I shouted. "The judge

gave me to Miss Carrie."

"You be quiet, boy. You have no say in this. You have no living kin so you are an orphan," sternly said Miss Greene.

"Now just a damn minute," Miss Carrie said. "Ben, go upstairs and brush your teeth and finish getting ready for school. Miss Greene, you come with me outside. I've got something to say to you."

She took the woman by the arm and rather forcefully led her out the door, slamming the door behind them.

I went upstairs and looked out the window. Miss Carrie was angry and seemed to be talking rapidly, every once in a while shaking her finger in the woman's face. Miss Greene just stood there with her legs wide and her mouth open.

After a short while Miss Carrie seemed to calm down, and Miss Greene seemed to relax. After a few more words Miss Carrie held out her hand and Miss Greene took it. Then Miss Greene got in her car and left.

Miss Carrie watched her drive off then folded her arms, turned and walked toward the house.

I hurried down the stairs as she entered through the door.

"What happened, Miss - I mean, Mimi?"

"Nothing, Sweety, we won't be bothered by her again. You will always live here and be safe here."

"But what did you say to her?" I asked.

"Nothing you need to be concerned with, dear Ben. I promise you've heard the last of her. I just told her how the cow ate the cabbage, as H. David said. Now get ready for school. You don't need to be late your first day back."

I put on my coat and cap and hugged Miss Carrie at the front door, then hopped on my bike and headed back to my old school, the Fabre Bluff Junior High.

When I arrived all the students had gone inside. I parked my bicycle in the bike rack and almost ran into the building. I rushed down the hall to what had been my old seventh grade home room prior to my time at the orphanage.

The room was empty! I had no idea what to do and was about to leave for the principal's office when all the students rushed out of the cloak room yelling "Welcome back, Ben" and all sorts of things. Even Miss Gaddy, the home room teacher, came out laughing. Amy led the way with Lonnie Joe, Harold and Jody closely behind.

The welcome excited me very much. After a few minutes Miss Gaddy said, "All right, students, take your seats. No more yelling or talking. Get your books out and ready yourselves for class. Ben, you come with me. We need to reassign you your books and supplies."

As I followed the teacher down the hall she said, "I understand you are living in the old Stephens home with Carrie Stephens. No one in this town, or this state for that matter, has ever seen her. How in the world did you ever become associated with her?"

"We played a trick on her on Halloween a long time ago. I knocked on her door because Lonnie and them dared me to. About the time I knocked they hit me with some eggs, and she opened the door and pulled me inside. She was real nice. She washed my clothes and let me clean up.

"Ever since then I've been going back to her house a lot. She's really nice and likes me a lot. The inside of her house is nicer than any house I've ever been in. She says I'm her little boy now, and she's gonna take care of me.

"She says now that she's got me she's gonna get out of the house and do things. She's even gonna buy a car, and Mr. Phillips is gonna teach her how to drive."

"Well I'll be," was all Miss Gaddy could say.

The school was no different than it had been prior to my time in the orphanage. All my friends were the same, but I had changed. Things that had been exciting before just seemed mundane now. Maybe, I thought, the orphanage had really changed me or maybe I was just growing up. I didn't know, but what I did know was that I didn't care to run with a crowd as I had earlier. Most of my free time was spent in and around my new home.

Miss Carrie was true to her word. She got out of the house almost daily. She even did her own shopping at Mr. Tucker's grocery having Marshal drive her in his Model A.

Spring came early, and by early March the days were warm enough to go outside without a coat. Marshal repaired the wrought iron fence as best he could, and one Saturday he and I painted it.

All the weeds inside the fence were removed, and the remaining grass was mowed, sometimes by Marshal and sometimes by me. Pushing the mower was hard work, but I enjoyed it, and Marshal frequently remarked how strong I was for my age.

Nothing could be done about the house due to lack of supplies because of wartime shortages. Even paint was in short supply.

In the middle of March, Marshal borrowed a mule and a plow, and we broke up a piece of ground between the house and the riverbank for a garden. Many vegetables were planted, and Lounicey anticipated lots of canning.

About that time Mr. Phillips came up in a used Studebaker he had found. Miss Carrie bought it and immediately started taking driving lessons from Mr. Phillips. She wouldn't let me ride with them but soon became proficient and then enjoyed taking me for rides when she could buy rationed gasoline.

Those days to me were wonderful, and it was obvious Miss Carrie felt the same.

School went well, although I was disappointed that I couldn't sit by Amy since we were seated alphabetically, she with the M's and I with the W's. However, during the thirty minute home room period and the late afternoon study hall we were able to sit side by side.

Amy remained sad for there had been no word of her father. Somehow her sadness made her more attractive to me.

On the last Saturday in March, Marshal and I were planting potatoes when we saw Amy running up the street yelling my name. I stopped what I was doing and ran to the fence to meet her.

"Ben," she said breathlessly, "Daddy is alive. Mama got

a letter from the Red Cross telling her he was in a German prison camp in Poland and was okay. At the same time she got a letter from the Army saying he had been freed and would be coming home soon."

I jumped the fence and hugged her. Miss Carrie, Lounicey and Marshal all gathered around us and hugged us both. Miss Carrie and Lounicey were crying.

In midmorning at school on Monday, April the thirtieth, the principal came into our room and announced that Hitler was dead. We all cheered, and the teacher let us run around the room, up and down the aisles. Harold and Lonnie even ran on the desk tops until Harold fell, and the teacher made them stop.

When I went home for lunch Miss Carrie said, "Ben, Marshal and I will have a surprise for you after school. Bring all your friends to see it."

"What is it, Mimi?" I asked.

"It wouldn't be a surprise if I told you. Just come and see."

As I rode my bike back to school, church bells were ringing, and sirens were going off all over town.

Nothing was accomplished in school that afternoon. By the time the last bell rang we were all headed to Miss Carrie's. Amy rode sideways on the cross-bars of my bicycle.

When we arrived we saw, hanging from a tree limb with his head in a noose, a life-size doll that looked just like Hitler. A crowd of adults were gathered, all singing patriotic songs.

It was some sight!

By now we had a phone. The number was 364.
Amy's number was 240, and we talked on the phone
each evening. We talked as long as we dared since Mrs.
McDonald was hoping for a call about her husband.

We were on the phone the night after Hitler's death
when Amy said, "I've got to go. Someone's at the door."

After about an hour the phone rang, and Miss Carrie
said, "Ben, it's Amy for you."

As I placed the receiver to my ear I heard Amy
exclaim, "Ben, it's Daddy. He's home, and he's all right.
Isn't it wonderful?"

"It sure is," I said, "I told you he'd be okay."

"You sure did! Oh, Ben, everything is going to be fine
now!"

The next Tuesday, May the eighth, the war in Europe
ended. We all rejoiced but Miss Carrie said, "It is so sad
President Roosevelt couldn't live to see it end."

I felt bad that I had forgotten all about his death three
weeks earlier.

Jack McDonald was a man of average height and build.
He looked taller than he was because of a rather gaunt

appearance due to malnutrition. Mary, his wife, and Amy dearly loved him as did he them.

Amy and Mary had come to love Fabre's Bluff, so the family decided to remain where they were rather than move to Little Rock. Jack was on terminal leave and was soon to be discharged from active duty but remain in the local National Guard to be able to reach retirement.

Amy was thrilled that they were staying in the Bluff; and, needless to say, so was I. Amy and I had become best friends, and her parents seemed to like me. As far as I was concerned, Amy would be my girlfriend forever.

Her parents welcomed me in their home at any time except when Amy was there alone. The porch was as far as I could get at those times.

Once while sitting with Amy on the porch swing her parents returned from a walk and approached us.

"Hi," said Amy.

"Hi, Mr. and Mrs. McDonald," I said.

The adults each sat in a wicker chair and, after small talk, Mr. McDonald said, "Ben, my boy, you've been here so much you're almost like family. Don't be so formal. Call us Mary and Jack. We'd like that."

"Yes sir, I'll try; but that doesn't seem right," I said.

"You have good manners, son; and we appreciate that. You've been raised right. That's obvious. But we want you to be comfortable around us and not so formal. We like you a lot," he winked at Amy and she blushed, "and it's obvious Amy likes you." Both adults laughed.

"So call us by our first names, please."

"Yes sir," I said. I had never known adults, other than colored people, who I had called by their first names.

The summer was moderate for the South. Marshal's garden thrived, and Miss Carrie shared the abundant vegetables with the McDonalds and, of course, with Lounicey and Marshal.

Marshal was able to scrounge enough paint to finish the fence, which really looked nice as did the grounds. The house still looked dilapidated due to wartime shortage of building material.

Miss Carrie became quite adept at driving the Studebaker and occasionally she would even let me drive.

On June twenty second, I became thirteen, and Miss Carrie had Amy, her parents, Lounicey and Marshal for a picnic in the back yard. She had a cake and homemade ice cream for dessert.

After the meal Marshal said, "Ben, I fixed you somethin' for your birthday. Come look."

We went to the edge of the ten foot high bluff bank and hanging far out on a large branch of a cotton willow tree was a long rope.

"You can take this here pole and hook this knobby stem on the rope and pull it to you, then swing way out and drop off in the river. You gotta promise you won't never do it without somebody be with you, though."

"Hey, thanks Marshal," I exclaimed.

"Let's go home and get our bathing suits, Amy. I want to try that," said Jack.

They ran home, hand in hand, the father and daughter. When they returned the three of us rode the rope and dropped into the river so much that our fingertips became wrinkled. I was never so happy.

The rest of June and July seemed to fly by. I spent part of my time helping Marshal with the garden and the lawn. The garden produced bountiful quantities of vegetables, and the lawn became lush due to more than ample rainfall.

One mid-July evening when the weather was unusually cool, Miss Carrie and I sat in the back yard watching fireflies. I was very relaxed and content. The stars were bright in the moonless sky and, along with the flickering of the fireflies and the gentle breeze, gave the night a surreal appearance.

"Mimi," I said, "I am so happy I live with you. I sometimes feel bad because I'm so happy, because if Daddy and Granny hadn't died I wouldn't be living here."

Tears began to run down my cheeks as I continued. "I didn't want them to die, but if they didn't I wouldn't be this happy. Is it wrong because I feel this way?"

She was quiet for a moment and then wiped my tears with her handkerchief. She said, "Sweety, you didn't cause them to die. Things happen which we have no control over, but we just have to make the best of them. I'm positive your daddy and grandmother and your mother too would want you to be happy. You can be sure they look down from heaven and are glad to see that you and I found each other.

"You know you make me happy too. So maybe somewhere in the scheme of things this was the way our lives were meant to be."

As we sat in silence we noticed the moon begin to rise in the east. She said, "Look at the big orange moon. It's that color because the sunlight from the other side of the world is filtered through the atmosphere. As it rises in the sky, there is less filtering of sunlight on it, and the moon will look smaller and will be white instead of orange. It will be so bright it will make most of the stars seem to go away, but they are still there. You just can't see them."

As the moon rose I could see what she was talking about, and I was impressed at how smart she was.

"Well, my big boy, it is time for bed but first I want to talk to you about something."

"Uh oh," I thought.

"All this summer I want you to play and have fun. That's what a thirteen year old boy should do. Of course you must help Marshal about the place some. But between now and next summer when you are fourteen, you will grow a lot. By that time you should have a summer job. Thurman Cato is a forester and manages all my timber. I want you to work for him and learn about pine trees and hardwood too. Someday all I have will be yours, and I want you to know about it from the bottom up."

I hadn't ever thought about that. "Yes ma'am," was all I could say.

On August the ninth all the newspapers and radio stations were full of the story of the atomic bomb dropping on Japan and a second one a few days later. By

the fourteenth the war was over, and the entire town
celebrated even more than at the end of the war against
Hitler. Marshal hung an effigy of Tojo in the same tree he
hung Hitler. A solid stream of cars drove by, their horns
blazing away.

Miss Carrie stayed inside and did not celebrate as
everyone else did. I found her sitting alone in the living
room.

"What's wrong, Mimi? Are you sick or something?" I
asked.

"No child, I'm just sad. I'm happy the war is over and
we can go back to normal living and, Lord knows, I don't
want any more of our boys to be killed or maimed; but I
grieve for all the innocent Japanese people, all the little
children, who were killed by the atomic bombs. War is so
cruel. I hope we never have another."

I hadn't thought about that, and I began to feel bad
about those people too. All I had thought about were
mean Japs. Now I realized that thousands of kids my age
and younger had been killed.

With the excitement of the war ending and all the
changes that brought about, time seemed to fly. The
trains and buses were full of returning men and women
of the armed services. Rationing went away; and Fabre's
Bluff, along with the rest of the nation, gradually returned
to normal.

Building supplies became available, and men were
available for work. Miss Carrie hired a builder, Harrison

Todd, to remodel the exterior of the house.

Over the next three months there was a drastic change in the appearance of the house. What had been a facade of faded wood, missing roof shingles, loose shutters and broken steps was by Christmas the picture of a lovely home. The walls were white, the roof dark gray, and the new shutters on all the windows were black. The wrought iron fence was black and upright with a front gate that swung free on its hinges. A sidewalk of stone led from the repaired front porch through the gate to the edge of the street.

In the side yard was a gazebo, all parts of which matched the corresponding parts of the house. It was the most beautiful house I had ever seen.

Christmas was wonderful. Miss Carrie gave me a new Schwinn bicycle. How she was able to find it and buy it I never knew. It was bright red.

As she gave it to me I never saw her look so happy, yet I felt as though there was some sadness in her. "Dear Ben," she said, "I want you to enjoy your red bike. You know it is traditional for boys to have red bikes and girls blue. Take good care of it and enjoy it but always be aware of the many less fortunate children who don't even have enough clothes, much less bicycles. Always be kind to them, for they need kindness and love."

That afternoon we had a great Christmas dinner attended by Mary, Jack and Amy as well as Lounicey and Marshal. After the meal we sang Christmas carols by the living room fireplace accompanied by Lounicey on the piano and Marshal on the banjo. I thought life could not be better.

Miss Carrie suggested I give my old bicycle to Marshal who could find a child who didn't have one, and I agreed. I loved my new bike and made sure it stayed clean and without scratches. I rode it for hours every day during the Christmas holidays.

One afternoon I was caught in a cold rain, and the wet bike, covered with mud, became coated with ice. I took it into the shed behind the house and got a bucket full of hot water from the kitchen and began washing the bike.

Miss Carrie came from the house and entered the shed just as I finished drying off the bicycle.

"I am so happy you like your bicycle, Ben; and I am very pleased to see you taking such good care of it," she said.

"Oh, Mimi, I just love it. It's the most beautiful bike I ever saw."

"It is beautiful," she said, "but I would like for you to remember something. Always know that beautiful things are not always good, but good things are always beautiful. Do you understand what that really means?"

I thought for a brief time and then replied, "I'm not sure, Mimi."

"Think of it this way, Sweety. There are beautiful people who are really bad, even evil. Their beauty is only skin deep. As you grow and mature you will have to look past their external beauty to recognize the true nature of the person who is hidden underneath the external beauty. But once you really see the true nature of a person and recognize that person as a good person, it doesn't matter what he looks like on the outside, he is beautiful."

I nodded my head affirmatively while thinking that Miss Carrie was the most beautiful person I knew.

The spring semester of the eighth grade passed very fast, and soon it was summer and time for my job in the woods. On the first Monday of the summer break, Miss Carrie woke me at five o'clock.

She said, "Wake up, sleepy head; it's time to get ready for work."

I crawled out of bed and while I wiped the sleep out of my eyes she tousled my head. "You need a haircut," she said, "either a haircut or dog license."

I dressed and met her and Lounicey at the breakfast table.

"Eat hearty, boy," said Lounicey. "You gonna be hot, tired and hungry by mid-day. I fixed you pimiento cheese sandwiches for your lunch. Mr. Cato, he'll have plenty ice water for you. It's gonna be hot, hotter'n where the boogerman stays, so you gonna need lots of water."

I ate two fried eggs, sunny side up, bacon, toast and jelly and washed it down with fresh milk. As I got up from the table Miss Carrie gave me a pair of snake chaps and said, "Ben, you're going to be in some deep woods. There may be snakes around, copperheads and rattlers most. You're not likely to see cottonmouths because you won't be around water. A snake won't likely bite you above the knee since you've grown so tall in the past year. You put these on just as soon as you get out of the car."

"Yes ma'am," I said as a car honked.

"There's Thurman," said Miss Carrie. "You do as he says, and you can learn a lot from him."

"Come on, boy," Mr. Cato yelled, "the woods is waitin'."

Thurman Cato was a wiry man weighing about a hundred and fifty and a little less than six feet tall. He had very short-cropped hair and was clean shaven.

On the way to the woods he described what my job would be. "Ben, you're gonna paint land lines this week with Junior. He'll show you what to do. Now you do what he says. He's colored, but he's still in charge and the boss of you."

"Yes sir, Mr. Cato," I said.

"Now drop that Mister shit, boy. Everbody calls me Cato. I don't like Mister, and I don't like Thurman. You call me Cato just like everybody else."

"Yes sir," I said.

"And drop that sir shit, too."

I could tell I was going to like him a lot.

When we arrived at a tall stand of pine trees, a black man was sitting on a stump at the edge of the road. As Cato stopped the truck the man got up and walked toward us.

"Ben, this is Junior," Cato said. "Junior, this is Ben Williams, Miss Carrie's boy. He's gonna be working with us this summer. Take him with you and teach him to mark land lines."

"Yeah sir," said Junior. "How do, Ben. Here, take this can and spray yourself good. The skeeters an' redbugs is some kinda bad."

"Hi, Junior," I said, "thanks." I took the can and sprayed my legs.

"Spray all over," said Junior. "Shut your eyes and hold your breath and spray your face good. Them skeeters loves that tender white skin. I seen a white boy once got bit so much his face swole up twiced it's normal size. His eyes swole shut an' I had to lead him outta the woods."

"Junior, stop shittin' the boy so much. Ben, you mind Junior, but watch out for his tall tales. I'll be back at noon. You got plenty of ice water, Junior?"

"Yeah-suh," replied Junior. "Ben, you got a dinner packed?"

"I've got two sandwiches Miss Carrie made."

"Good, if you don't eat both of um, I'll eat one."

Cato left, and I followed Junior into the woods. He was tall and lanky and had very large feet. There was a little gray at his temples, but I had no idea how old he was. He sang as he walked.

I walked behind him and carried a machete. Junior had a very long, but slow, stride.

We arrived at our starting point, and Junior taught me how to use the machete to cut a small path. He followed behind dabbing paint along the way.

After about half an hour Junior said, "Slow down, boy, we got all day an' then some. You need to learn you ain't gotta do a job in one day. The way you're hurryin', you'll be wore out by dinner. The pay gonna be the same whether you get through today or not."

Cato said he was my boss, so I did as he said. I was glad he gave me the mosquito dope, because they really were swarming.

We established and marked land lines for the rest of

the week. At quitting time on Friday, Cato handed me a check for thirty-two dollars and fifty cents. That was sixty-five cents an hour for fifty hours work.

I thought I was rich.

For the rest of the summer I worked exclusively with Junior, who I came to like and admire very much. He was funny and always had tall stories to tell. He took care of me and made sure I didn't do too much and tire myself out. When a task seemed too much for me, he made me sit down, and he did both of our jobs.

Most of the summer was spent cutting and marking land lines, but I learned much more. I watched workers dropping trees and removing limbs. I knew which trees were to be cut into billets for the paper mill and which were to be cut into logs for the sawmill.

By the end of the first month I knew the difference between pine and the various hardwoods. I developed an appreciation for wildlife and the importance of streamside management.

After ten weeks I had earned three hundred and seventy-five dollars, most of which I had saved, but some I had spent on Amy and me.

In those ten weeks I only saw one snake, a harmless water snake.

By the time I was fifteen and ready to start the tenth grade I had grown to just over six feet tall and had bulked up to a hundred seventy-five pounds.

I wasn't interested in sports, nor did I run with a crowd since most of my old friends played football and basketball. I read a lot and spent a great deal of my time with Amy.

During that school year I began to have feelings for Amy that I didn't understand. She was more than just my childhood girlfriend. She was more than a friend. I didn't know how I felt, I just knew it was pleasant yet confusing.

One afternoon as we were walking home from school I impulsively took her hand in mine, and she did not resist. We walked all the way to her house hand in hand, and I had a warm, comfortable feeling that I had never before experienced.

At her front door we said goodbye, and she suddenly kissed me on the cheek, turned and ran inside. I was stunned.

I walked home feeling pleasantly strange. When I walked through the back door into the kitchen, Miss Carrie was sitting at the table.

She must have noticed I was different, because she said, "Sweety, come sit with me and tell me about it."

"Tell you about what?" I said as I sat down.

"Tell me about what brought on that goofy look on your face," she replied with a smile.

"What goofy look?" was all I could say.

"That look that says I think I'm in love, and I don't know what to do about it. You want to tell someone, but you don't know how. Remember, Ben, I was young once; and I had my Floyd. I'm not too old to remember how it felt."

So I told her about the afternoon with Amy.

"Tell me how you feel about it," she said.

"I don't know what to say," I replied.

"Well, let me see if I can describe it," she said. "Does it feel something like you feel when you awaken on a very cold morning with lots of cover on you all pulled up under your chin, and you're warm and cozy, so much so that you don't want to get up?"

"Yes ma'am, I guess it does."

"Well, Sweety, what started out as friendship has blossomed into love. You and Amy are in love. You're both just fifteen, but you are not too young to love each other in the boy-girl, man-woman way. Don't ever doubt that and don't ever let anyone cast a doubt on it. You are both old enough.

"You remember when I told you that everything that is good is beautiful. Well, your love for Amy and hers for you is good and is beautiful. Hold onto it and treasure it, and you can have a wonderful life together. I know. I had my Floyd for a short time, but I have loved him forever. I hope you have Amy, or rather you and Amy have each other, for the rest of your lives."

I was amazed at how wise Miss Carrie was, and I knew she was right. I was in love for the first time, and hopefully it would last forever.

The three years of high school seemed to fly by. Amy and I were together almost every day. She was active in most of the extracurricular activities, but I was not. We

both studied hard. Amy made nothing but A's, but I had
an occasional B.

Summers were spent in the woods with Thurman Cato.
I learned to operate various machines such as front-end
loaders and was even allowed to drive log trucks to the
lumber yards, but I was never allowed to use a chainsaw
to cut down trees. Cato said that was due to strict orders
from Miss Carrie.

I learned to identify the various hardwood trees and
knew which size of a pine tree was good for cutting into
billets for the paper mill and which size was to be cut
for the sawmill. I loved the woods and often thought of
the line from the poem, Evangeline – This is the forest
primeval.

I also came to a sincere appreciation of wildlife and
vowed never to be a hunter for I knew I could never kill
such beautiful animals, even for food.

On Miss Carrie's orders I was allowed to visit her
producing oil wells and study them, but she never allowed
me to work in the oil fields. She said it was just too
dangerous.

So by age eighteen Amy and I graduated from high
school. Amy was valedictorian, and I was an honor
graduate. Her parents and Miss Carrie were extremely
proud of us.

The year was nineteen fifty; and, at eighty-four, Miss
Carrie was beginning to show her age. Her mind was
as sharp as ever, but physically she was beginning to
deteriorate. She visited her doctor regularly and took
the medicine he prescribed faithfully, but the years were
beginning to take their toll.

Amy and I were more in love than ever, and that
summer we became lovers. We were committed to each

other and resolved to marry at an appropriate age, but passion got the better of us, and we succumbed to it.

Miss Carrie insisted on my attending college and would hear of nothing but the University of Arkansas in Fayetteville. Aware of how weak she was, I wanted to go to school closer to home and preferred Southern State College, thirty-five miles to the south of the Bluff.

She could not be persuaded to the contrary, so I applied for and was accepted for admission to the University in Fayetteville. Amy, wanting to be with me as I wanted to be with her, also was accepted by the University.

As September drew near I was developing separation anxiety, and I could sense the same in Miss Carrie.

One evening, when the air was pleasant with a full moon on the rise and a gentle breeze, Miss Carrie asked me to sit with her for a while in the gazebo.

We sat in the swing, gently swaying back and forth, when she said, "Ben, I'm an old lady and a weak and tired one at that. Had you not come into my life I'm sure I would have died long ago. I absolutely love you being with me, and I hate to see you leave. But, Sweety, there is a time for everything in this life; and it is time for you to go."

"Aw, Mimi," I started.

"Hush, child, now hear me out," she said. I could see a faraway look in her eyes, but I stopped and prepared to listen.

"You have lived with me for over five years, and I think of you as my child. I want for you all that is good and beautiful in this life. I want you to be educated and experience college life. I am old, and I know arithmetic. Four years added to my eighty-four and I might not live to see you graduate, but that is what I want for you. That is what I know is best for you. That is what I insist upon.

"Do that for me but also for you, and you will make this old woman happy. Promise me!"

I didn't want to leave her, the nearest thing to a mother I had ever known; but what could I say? "I promise," I said, with tears in my eyes.

She pulled me to her and held me for the longest. Then she backed away slightly, laughed, and said, "Okay, that's settled. Now you hold onto Amy and love her and never let her go. When you marry her, and you will, I hope you have a little girl and name her Evangeline and call her Eve. I plan to live long enough to hold that baby."

"If we have a little girl, that will be her name, although I would prefer to name her Carlotta."

"No, not Carlotta," she said. "Carrie will be okay, but for your second little girl," she said, with a twinkle in her eye.

"If it's a boy, I want to name him Floyd," I said.

She said nothing but turned away from me so that I would not see her cry. After about a minute she said, "I would like that."

Toward the end of August Miss Carrie woke me early on a Saturday morning.

"Get dressed and come down for breakfast," she said. "I

want you to go somewhere with me."

"Go where?" I asked.

"It's a surprise," she said, as she started down the stairs.

When I entered the kitchen, Sweet Pea said, "Sit yourself, boy. Here comes some eggs an' sausage an' biscuits, an' they's hot."

Miss Carrie sat at the table drinking coffee and grinning.

"Hurry up, Sweety, we've got business to transact," she commanded.

I hurriedly finished my breakfast, got up from the table and followed Miss Carrie to the door.

"Have you got the keys to the old Studebaker?" she asked. When I nodded affirmatively, she said, "We're going in the Studebaker. You drive."

She had bought herself a light blue forty-seven Roadmaster Buick and had turned the Studebaker over to me a couple of years earlier.

As we walked to the car I asked, "Where are we going, Mimi?"

She replied, "Hush, boy, and just go where I tell you."

We had driven in silence for several blocks when she said, "Stop here."

It was the Chevrolet dealership in front of which was parked a new, bright red, nineteen-fifty Chevrolet Bel Air.

"How do you like that, Ben?" she asked.

"It's a beauty," I replied.

"It's yours," she said, with the largest grin I had ever seen on her face.

"No, Mimi, the Studebaker is fine. You don't need to buy that for me."

"Too late. I've already bought it and put it in your

name. The Studebaker belongs to Mr. Summers now."

I didn't know what to say. I knew she loved me as I loved her, but why had she lavished so much on me? She was giving me a college education, she had given me a home, now she was giving me a brand new car. Why was I so lucky? I had no idea.

Around the first of September after finishing dinner we lingered at the table. Lounicey had cleared the table. Miss Carrie and I were finishing our iced tea when Lounicey came in.

She said, "Miss Carrie, I've finished with the dishes. You need anything else?"

"No, Sweet Pea. Go on home. Pleasant dreams."

"Yes'um," she replied, as she looked at me and winked, then turned and left.

"I just love Lounicey and Marshal too. They have been so good to me. Until you came along they were the only family I had."

"I know," I said.

After a short period of silence I began to rise from my chair.

"Keep your seat for awhile, Sweety. Let's talk." She looked as though she wanted to tell me something. She started to speak, then looked way and gazed out the window.

Finally she said, "It's lovely this evening, but it's a shame it's so hot and humid. Thank goodness for our fans. But enough small talk. You've said nothing of where you're going to live at school. And what about rush week and the fraternities?"

"Mimi, I don't want to live in a crowded room with two or three other boys. I'm sort of a loner as you probably know. If I could find a small apartment that didn't cost any more than a dorm room, would you mind if I rented it and lived alone?"

"If that's what you want, then do it. Don't worry about the cost."

"No ma'am, I don't want you to have to pay more than dorm room would cost."

"You silly boy! What good is my money if I don't spend it? Here's what I'm going to do. I'm going to pay your tuition and books, and I'm going to send you a hundred and twenty-five dollars a month to live on. Do you think that is enough?"

"Oh, yes ma'am, more than enough," I replied.

"So be it then, Sweety. I'm going to miss you something terrible, but time passes, and life goes on. You have become a man. It's time for you to take the next step. In four years you'll be back here running all my affairs.

"Now I know you're worried about me. You're afraid I'll go back into my shell." I nodded yes. "Well, I won't. I promise. I've come to enjoy being out and around, church and all. I love my Buick. I may even come up to Fayetteville to see you – to make sure you're eating right and keeping your apartment straight," she said. Then we both laughed.

September the fifth dawned cold but clear. My car
was packed, and I was ready to leave by six o'clock. Amy's
parents were to take her, and I was to follow.

Lounicey and Marshal were there to see me off. As I
stood by the open door of my car I noticed Lounicey wipe
her eyes with her apron and Marshal looking away. Miss
Carrie had a smile on her face and a tear in her eye.

She gave me a hug and whispered in my ear,
"Godspeed, dear Ben. Remember the old witch loves you."

Then she backed away and said, "Remember, young
man, pretty is as pretty does. Now get gone!"

I turned quickly, got in the car and started toward the
McDonald's house. I didn't want them to see me cry.

The trip to Fayetteville took seven hours since we
stopped at Clarksville for a sandwich. I followed Amy
and her parents to Holcomb Hall, the freshman girls'
dormitory, and told Jack and Mary goodbye. I gave Amy a
hug and left for the registrar's office.

The clerk got me registered for school and instructed
me where to go to register for class at the end of rush
week. When I told her I wanted to find a small apartment
rather than live in a dormitory, she gave me a list of
apartments for rent.

I got lucky on my first attempt. On the side of a
mathematics professor's home was a small two room wing
that had been where his mother had lived until she died. It
was furnished and had a living room and bedroom. There
was a tiny kitchen and slightly larger bathroom. The rent

was only twenty-five dollars a month, and utilities were included in the rent.

Mrs. Shaver, the owner, gave me rules I must follow if they rented it to me. "Young man," she said, "There can be no drinking or smoking and no partying. You may have guests but no women overnight."

I said, "Mrs. Shaver, I don't drink or smoke. I don't party. I like to be alone. But I do have a girlfriend. Her name is Amy, and her parents just moved her into Holcomb Hall. She is a very nice girl. She may visit me here but only to talk or study. She will never spend the night here, I promise. "

"Well, I guess that will be all right," she said.

We shook hands, and I gave Mrs. Shaver twenty-five dollars and moved in. The apartment was entered through a tiny portico into the living room, which was darkly paneled. There was a small fireplace in which was a gas stove, the only heat in the place. A tiny kitchenette was to the left past a small dining alcove. The bedroom was small and had a chest of drawers and a double bed with a straw mattress. The bathroom had a sink, commode and small tub. There was no shower. The place was perfect for me.

The McDonalds helped Amy move in Holcomb and get settled. Amy was in a small, crowded three girl room. After Amy was settled, her parents came by my apartment on Ozark Street to tell me goodbye.

Jack said, "Ben, I know you care deeply for Amy, and I know she cares just as much for you. Please watch out

for her and phone us if she needs anything. Here is twenty
dollars to get a phone. I'd feel more comfortable if you had
a phone."

"You don't need to do that, Jack. I plan to get a phone
in the next day or two," I replied.

"No, take it. I want you to. So does Mary. I'll be
insulted if you don't."

So I took the twenty, and we shook hands. Mary gave
me a hug. As we walked to their car Jack turned and, with
a stern look, said, "Don't you two get in trouble. Do you
know what I mean?"

I felt my face begin to flush and my ears burn. "Yes
sir," I said. "I know what you mean."

The fall semester went by fast. Amy and I attended all
the football games and saw movies together. We usually
ate out after the games on Saturday nights.

Frequently Amy cooked our weeknight meals at my
apartment and then we studied. We were careful to leave
the lights on and the window shades up, because we
suspected Mrs. Shaver was watching us. Occasionally
when we knew the Shavers were away we made love, but
that occurred infrequently.

By the Thanksgiving break we had begun to talk
of marriage. We were only eighteen, and I knew that
she, being eighteen, could marry without her parents'
permission. The law at that time required the male to be
twenty-one, so Miss Carrie would have to sign for me. I
knew she would, but I didn't want to marry without Amy's

parents' permission.

On the drive to Fabre's Bluff the day before Thanksgiving Amy brought the subject up.

"Ben, I know you love me, and you know I love you. If we were in our twenties we would already be married. So why not now? I'm tired of living in a little bitty room with two other girls. We could live in your apartment. I don't want to join a sorority, and you obviously aren't considering a fraternity."

"I feel the same way, but let's wait until summer to get just a little older. I'll talk to Jack then."

She said, "Pull over and stop the car."

I did, and we embraced and kissed.

When we reached Fabre's Bluff I dropped Amy off at her house, exchanged pleasantries with her parents and hurried home. When I arrived at the rear of the house Miss Carrie, followed by Lounicey and Marshal, came out to greet me. Miss Carrie was walking with the aid of a cane.

"Why the cane, Mimi?" I asked, after a long hug.

"'I'm just a little unsteady on my feet, that's all. It's nothing. I just don't want to take a chance on falling at my age. Look at you! You've put on weight."

"Lots of baloney and cheese, and Amy cooks several nights a week."

I could tell she wanted to ask me something, but she said nothing.

When we were out of earshot of Lounicey she said,"

Ben, Amy isn't sleeping over with you at the apartment, is she?

"No ma'am," I said. That was not a lie. Even though we were lovers she had never spent the night with me.

After supper Lounicey and Marshal left and Miss Carrie said, "It's a lovely evening, Sweety, let's sit on the porch a bit."

We sat in the porch swing and gently swayed back and forth. She took my hand and for the longest said nothing.

Holding my right hand in her left she softly rubbed the back of my hand with her right hand. Finally she said, "Sweety, believe it or not, I was young once. I know how young lovers feel, and I know what they do. Remember, I had my Floyd once. There will come a time when you want to get married. There may come a time when you need to get married."

I started to say something, but she held up her hand and said, "Hush now. Let me finish. When either of those times come, and you need help or advice, you and Amy come to me. Always know I am on your side."

I didn't know what to say, so I said nothing. At that moment I loved her more than ever.

Well, that time did come. On a Friday afternoon shortly before the end of the school year I came home to find Amy sitting on my portico. Tears were in her eyes.

"Ben, I've missed two periods. I went to the doctor today, and he thinks I'm about six weeks pregnant. He can't be sure, though. I haven't been sick or anything like that, but I know I am."

I took her in my arms and said, "Well, don't cry about it. We'd planned to get married later this summer, so we'll just do it now. I love you, Amy. You know you're the only girl I've ever been with, the only girl I have ever loved or will love. I'm ready for marriage, baby or no baby."

"But my parents will kill me," she cried.

"No they won't. They love you. Besides, Miss Carrie will help us with them."

"Miss Carrie will hate me," she cried.

"No she won't. She loves you. She implied last Thanksgiving that if this happened we should come to her, and she would help us."

"She actually said that?" Amy asked, with an incredulous look on her face.

"In so many words, but I knew what she meant."

The next week we drove home and went directly to Miss Carrie's house. She met us on the porch. She looked at us both for a minute, then grinned and said, "Let me be the first to congratulate you."

Then she hugged us both. I couldn't help but laugh.

"Come on," she said, "I'll help you tell your parents."

We drove in silence to the McDonald's house. Amy looked worried, and her hands were trembling slightly. When we parked in front of the house and got out of the car, Jack and Mary emerged from the house with a surprised look on their faces. I was sure they were wondering why Miss Carrie was with us.

"What's wrong?" asked Mary, as she hugged Amy, who remained silent.

Jack looked at me as if he were expecting an answer.

"We have some news," I said, as we all took a seat on the porch.

"Spill it," said Jack rather tensely. "Do you all need to get married?"

"We want to," Amy replied.

Miss Carrie spoke up and said, "If you all will let me speak my peace, I would like to tell you what I think."

Jack nodded affirmatively; Mary just looked at her hands folded in her lap.

Miss Carrie continued, "We all know these young people have been best friends for years. We also know that they have come to love each other and that some day they would marry. There is a possibility that a pregnancy is involved; they don't know for sure. However, they want to marry before they know, one way or the other. They want to marry because they want to and not because they have to. That's why they want to marry now."

I knew it was a white lie, because we were sure, but I thought it was a good lie.

Jack and Mary looked at each other for the longest without responding. Finally Mary looked at us and said, "I think a marriage this week is a wonderful idea. I love both of you, and I know Jack does too. I'm also glad that you want to marry because you love each other and not because you think you must.

"And, anyway, if there is a baby, we will love it. Many a good marriage has started with a baby due."

Jack said, "Amen" and laughed as he pulled Amy into his arms.

I looked at Miss Carrie. She had tears in her eyes.

We applied for our license as soon as the county clerk's office opened, got our blood tests and began the three day waiting period. During that time we had daily counseling sessions with the Methodist minister. Amy stayed with her parents, and I stayed at my home with Miss Carrie.

When the waiting period was up we had a quiet wedding in the chapel of the church attended only by Miss Carrie, the McDonalds, Lounicey, Marshal, and Mr. Phillips.

After the ceremony we all went to Miss Carrie's. Lounicey had made a wedding cake, and Marshal had churned homemade vanilla ice cream.

Miss Carrie had iced down a magnum of champagne. She poured us all a glass but only put a very small amount in Amy's glass, which she handed to her with a twinkle in her eye.

"I want to propose a toast," she said. "To this young man whom I have loved since I found him on my porch covered with eggs, and to his bride whom I also love as if she were my own. May you have a long happy marriage and may you have many healthy children."

We all raised our glasses and then drank the contents. Amy only took a very small sip which her mother noticed with a smile on her face. I knew Jack and Mary were fully aware, and I was glad.

After a short honeymoon at Hot Springs financed by Miss Carrie as a wedding gift, we returned to Fabre's Bluff. We spent the night at Amy's house and then went back to Fayetteville to find a larger apartment.

We found a nice apartment two blocks from the campus, bid Mrs. Shaver goodbye and moved into our first home. I carried Amy across the threshold.

Both of us enrolled in summer school. Miss Carrie continued to finance us but increased my monthly stipend to two hundred dollars.

The pregnancy passed slowly but uneventfully, and on New Year's Day at one in the morning our baby was born. It was a girl. She weighed a little over seven pounds and was healthy, as was Amy.

As soon as the sun was up I phoned first Amy's parents and then Miss Carrie.

"Hello," Miss Carrie said.

"Mimi, it's me. The baby is here and healthy, as is Amy."

I paused, and she said, "All right, Ben, you've had your fun. Boy or girl?"

"A girl, seven pounds. Her name is Evangeline Mary Williams, and she will be called Eve."

There was a pause, and I thought I heard a sob. Finally she said, "God bless you, dear Ben. I love you so."

"We love you, too, Mimi; and little Eve will, too."

Both mother and daughter did well, and were allowed to go home after six days. Miss Carrie had sent me five hundred dollars to buy all the furniture needed for Eve's room.

When Eve was two weeks old, Jack and Mary drove to Fayetteville to see their granddaughter. They brought Miss Carrie with them. It was the first time Miss Carrie had been out of Ouachita County since she was a little girl.

All three of them took to the baby immediately and she to them as only a newborn can.

The McDonalds were to stay in the Washington Hotel, but Miss Carrie was to stay with us. We arranged for her to have our bedroom, and Amy and I were to sleep on a pallet in Eve's room. Miss Carrie protested but in the end agreed on the arrangement.

That evening after Jack and Mary left Miss Carrie rocked the baby.

She said, "In all my eighty-five years I don't believe I have ever seen such a beautiful baby. I can't tell you how much I appreciate your naming her Evangeline."

"We were happy to, Mimi," said Amy. "It's a lovely name."

"Mimi," I said, "why did you want us to name her that? Was it because you loved the poem so much?"

"I do love the poem; it's my favorite," she replied, "but that's not the only reason. I just love the name. I'll tell you more someday, but I'm not ready to now."

Leave it to Mimi, I thought, she just loved to be mysterious.

Amy decided not to return to school, because she

wanted to be able to be with Eve full time.

Over the next two years the three of us traveled back to Fabre's Bluff often because we wanted Eve to know her family from early childhood. One trip we would stay with the McDonalds and alternate trips at Miss Carrie's.

Eve loved being with Miss Carrie, and Miss Carrie enjoyed her. She had Marshal build a swing for her in the side yard and also a sandbox for her to play in. She would not let her play in the backyard for fear of her falling off the bluff into the river. Any time Eve was to play outside someone had to be with her.

We enjoyed staying at Miss Carrie's because we knew that it would be our home after I graduated.

We were amused at how Miss Carrie and Lounicey doted on Eve and how they competed with each other for her attention.

Over the years Miss Carrie's health began to deteriorate mainly due to the changes of aging. By the winter of fifty three-fifty four when she was eighty-eight, she needed a walker fulltime. Lounicey was staying with her ten to twelve hours a day, and a visiting nurse sat with her each night.

That winter my life was to change forever.

At six o'clock in the morning on January the fifth, I was awakened by the telephone. It was Lounicey.

"Hello," I said.

"Is that you, Ben? It's me, Lounicey." I could tell she was crying.

"It's me, Lounicey. What's wrong?"

"Oh, Ben, it's terrible. Miss Carrie fell last night and broke her hip. She in the hospital. The doctor say she dyin'. He say she got blood clots in her lungs. She in a coma, Ben. You gotta come. The doctor say she not gonna wake up, but if she do, she gonna want to see you."

"Lounicey, I'll be on my way just as quick as I can get dressed. It'll take me about six hours. I'll try to get there by early afternoon."

"We're going with you," exclaimed Amy, now wide awake. "I'll get dressed quick, and we can let Eve nap on the way. I'll ride in the back seat with her."

"Okay, but hurry," I said.

There had been snow and ice for the past two days, so I worried about the road condition, particularly through the mountains; but the road was clear all the way to Alma.

The trip was uneventful, and we pulled up to the hospital in Fabre's Bluff a little after two.

"You hurry on in, Ben. I'll take Eve to Mom and Daddy's and then come back."

I entered the hospital, asked for and got directions to Miss Carrie's room and rushed up the stairs to find Marshal sitting in the hall by her door.

"She still alive, Ben, but she unconscious. Lounicey with her," he said.

When I saw her I was shocked. She was barely breathing. Lounicey had been crying.

A nurse came in and said, "You must be Ben. She called for you before she lost consciousness. She has had a major pulmonary embolus. The doctor said it's just a matter of time. She can't survive. I'm so sorry."

When the nurse left Lounicey said, "Ben, I got somethin' Miss Carrie asked me to give to you once she gone. She dyin' and ain't gonna wake up, so I'm gonna give it to you now."

She handed me a large manila envelope and said, "I'm goin' out an' sit with Marshal. You needs to be alone with her. Call me if you needs me."

I looked at the envelope for the longest before opening it. Finally opening it I found a rather long letter. It read:

My Dear Ben:

By the time you read this I will have died and hopefully have gone to heaven to be with Floyd. Don't be sad. I had a good life, particularly since an egg-covered little boy knocked on my door many years ago.

I hope you know how much I love you. You were truly a joy to me and a blessing from God.

When H. David gives you a copy of my will, you will see that I have left Lounicey and Marshal well taken care of. I gave them their home many years ago, and I have left a sizable amount of money in trust for them for the rest of their lives. When the last one dies, what is left of their trust will go to their church.

Everything else I own will go to you – the house, all the furniture et cetera, all the timberland and oil wells, they are yours. Amy gets all my personal effects. But of course, all that is yours will be hers as well since I know how much you two love each other. I know you will never part.

You are now a very rich man. Use your wealth wisely and always remember those less fortunate than you.

Finish your education and move back to Fabre's Bluff and raise my dear little Eve in this house that I love. I hope she and your other children will spend many hours swinging on the rope Marshal hung in the tree for you and the little swing he made for Eve.

Now I want to finish the story I told you about Floyd

and me. You remember I told you we were to be married when I was eighteen, but he was killed in a runaway of his two-horse buggy on his way to me from Old Washington.

What I didn't tell you was that I was two months pregnant with his child. That was why he was in such a hurry to get here. Had he not run his team so fast he probably would not have been killed. So you see I always felt responsible for his death.

I was distraught and had some sort of breakdown. All my hair fell out, and when it grew back it was snow white.

When Papa found out about the pregnancy he was angry and ashamed. He confined me to the house until the baby was born. Lounicey's mother, Elnora, was the midwife who delivered my little girl. I named her Evangeline and called her Eve, but Papa wouldn't let me keep her.

When she was three days old, Papa took her from me and gave her to a childless couple who adopted her. When my baby was three, Elnora told me where she was, and Lounicey kept me up with how she was doing through the years. Elnora made me promise never to tell anyone what I knew about little Eve. I have kept that promise until now.

I was so heartbroken that I just became the recluse that I remained until that day in court when I came to lay my claim on you.

The couple that adopted my little girl named her Narcissa and called her Narcie.

You see, my dearest boy, I love you for two reasons — because you are you and because by birth I am your great-grandmother.

With all my love,
Mimi

I was stunned, but now everything made sense to me. Through tears I looked at Miss Carrie.

Her eyes were open, and I heard her whisper, "Dear Ben." Those were the last words I ever heard her say.

Reading Group Extras

A Note from the Author

I was born and raised in Newport, Arkansas. We were a family of four. My father was a lawyer, my mother was a homemaker. My younger brother Phillip and I were typical small-town boys in the 1950s. Phillip would grow up to be a lawyer; I was always expected to be a lawyer and planned to be one until our senior yearbook came out a month before graduation. Here is an anecdote I have never told before, about what put the idea of becoming a doctor in my mind. Intending a spoof in the senior class prophesy, my friend Sarah wrote, "Judson Hout will be a great surgeon and a rival of the famous Mayo Brothers. Even now he can cut a watermelon open." On hot Arkansas summer nights, some of us were known to steal the occasional watermelon. Sarah put the idea in my head, and one day I just said, "Why not?!"

The home in which I grew up was about a hundred feet north of the White River bridge. South of the bridge was Chastain's Addition, a poorer area, where three of my closest friends (Carlos, Gene and Leroy) lived. Those were idyllic days. We wore no shoes in the summer (except for Sundays), explored and played out of doors from breakfast until dark. Often wee could be found playing on the bridge, riding bicycles anywhere we wished, chasing the ice wagon in hopes of receiving a chip to lick. Newport, Arkansas was a great place to grow up in the 1950s.

I graduated from Newport High School in 1953, attended the University of Arkansas in Fayetteville and graduated from the University of Arkansas School of Medicine in Little Rock. My residency in Tulsa went quickly and then for two years I served as Medical Officer

on the Air Force at Bossier Base, a Defense Atomic
Support Agency base, in Shreveport, Louisiana. The
rest of my life has been spent in Camden, Arkansas,
where I practiced Family Medicine full time until 2011.
For the past 21 years I have been married to my high
school sweetheart, Carolyn, and together we have a
blended family of six children, their spouses and sixteen
grandchildren.

I love poetry and often try to weave certain of my
favorites into my novels. The reader will note the
prominent part the poem "Evangeline" plays in this novel.
My wife is an avid reader who leans toward mysteries.
Still, she is my best editor and critic.

This book, *Miss Carrie*, came to me all at once like a
bolt of lightning while I was driving alone one day to Little
Rock. When I arrived at home, I immediately wrote the
last chapter while it was fresh in my mind. Over the next
couple of months I wrote the rest of the novel.

Q & A With Author Judson Hout

Q: Is any of this story true?

A: No, it is totally fiction, a product of my imagination.

Q: Are any of the characters based on real people?

A: No, not in any literal sense. Two "old ladies" who live next door to us when I was growing up inspired parts of the title character, but other elderly women played parts in her formation as well. Of those two who made an early impression, one was a widow and the other an old maid. They were named Narcissa and Carrie. Both were Episcopalians, and my father and I took them to the midnight service every Christmas Eve. They were lovely ladies. I borrowed their names for this story, but the characters in the story are composites of many who influenced me over the years.

Q: Why do you think this kind of story is popular today?

A: I think that even today, with all the movies and books about crime, car chases, vampires and murder, people still like a traditional, old-fashioned heart-warming story about good, kind people. People still like to shed a happy tear or two.

Q: How did you come up with the name, Fabre's Bluff, for the locale of the story?

A: The original name of Camden, Arkansas was *Ecore Fabre,* French for Fabre's Bluff. I wanted a fictional name for the town, and I thought Fabre's Bluff sounded sufficiently mysterious.

**Q: Have you borrowed any other names of real
people in the story?**

A: No, but the lawyer H. David Phillips was chosen to
honor my late brother, Phillip David Hout.

**Q: Could the locale of this story be anywhere other
than South Arkansas?**

A: Of course it could, but I have live almost all my life in
Arkansas and love this state. I feel like I honor the place I
live by making it the locale of my stories.

Q: Do you have any other books in the works?

A: I have an idea for another book, but I haven't so far
been able to get it right in my mind. Maybe I've succumbed
to writer's block; I don't know. Hopefully the full story will
come to me soon.

Q: When you write do you dictate or type?

A: I do all my writing in longhand on yellow legal tablets
and then have it typed.